New Dawning International Bookfair

Presents

The Televangelist

A two part novel of Greed and Lust

By

Dee Dawning

Copyright © Dee Dawning 2010

Book One

The Bastard Preacher

Chapter One –Missy

*When it comes to the income of the ministry, I have no
problem talking about it or what happens to the money.*
Rev. Benny Hinn

**Tyler Texas, Summer 1988, Lone Star
Drive-in Theater**

Cheryl yanked his hand off her breast, pushed out
of his grasp and slid against the passenger door of his
twenty-year-old Pontiac.

"Dammit, Jamie Lee. I'm not going to screw you. I
came here to watch a movie."

Jamie Lee posed that hangdog look, for which
he'd became so well known when he didn't get his
way. "C'mon Cherrie, you know you'd really enjoy it."

"I might, but despite your colored reputation, I
didn't think you'd try to seduce me within an hour of
our first date."

His jaw tensed and his lips tightened. "Just how many dates would it take to get into them bright red panties?"

She looked down. Shaking her head, she pulled the hem of her short skirt down. "I don't know. There's no set time. Maybe a couple of months."

His eyes bored into her. "A couple months!" His hand struck the dashboard. "Fuck that! Cherrie, you eva hear that saying about the hereafta."

Cheryl's brow furrowed as she narrowed her blue eyes. "No, I can't say I have."

"It goes like this. If you're not hereafta what I'm hereafta, you're gonna still be hereafta I'm long gone." Jamie Lee snarled, "I'm going to the snack bar for sodas and popcorn then to the restroom to get a rubber. When I come back I wanna see your lacy red panties and bra draped around the car's shift knob or not only will this be our first date, it'll be our *last* date." Spittle flew from his mouth. "Now here's the good part. If we do it, everything will be cool. Everyone will suspect we did it, but no one will know for sure, 'cause I won't say anything. However, if you don't, they won't have to suspect because I'll tell everyone you are one hot fuck."

As Cheryl cast a hateful stare, she spoke through gritted teeth. "You asshole."

He opened the door. His jaw slackened while his lips curled into a malicious grin. "That's right sweetheart." After getting out then shutting the door, he leaned in and laughed. "But I gotta tell ya. They usually call me a son-of-a-bitch." He pulled away still

The Televangelist I

laughing and slapped the roof of the car before heading toward the refreshment center.

Ten minutes later, a condom safely ensconced in the change pocket of his jeans and carrying a large container of popcorn and two drinks, he noticed the interior light on. He picked up his pace. A few feet from the car, he saw the passenger door standing wide open. "What the fu…" The bitch wasn't there. He rushed to the door and found a handwritten note on the console by the shift knob. He set the cardboard tray on the passenger seat and snatched the note.

You're right. You're not an asshole. Son-of-a-bitch either. You're worse. You're a cocksucker. Go ahead and tell everyone what a hot fuck I am. I'll be the most popular girl on the campus, but while you're telling them what a great fuck I am, I'll be telling them what a bum fuck you are.

She signed the note with a happy face.

Jamie Lee crumbled and tossed the note inside, then thrust the open door, shut. He seldom had anyone say no to him. He didn't like it. Jamie Lee kicked the rear quarter panel. *She can't be far away. I'll catch her and then we'll see who sucks cocks.* He booted the tire, dashed to the driver's side, jumped in, started the engine, and drove off. The car wobbled as the steering wheel pulled left.

After driving a hundred feet, he stopped and jumped out. "Yiiaaeeee!" he screamed. *Fucking flat tire.* He reached in, took the refreshment tray, then flung it as far he could throw. He lurched around the car

The Televangelist I

cussing and kicking it. Finally, he settled down, opened the trunk to retrieve the spare.

Jamie Lee, you know better than that. Things work out much better when you talk someone into something rather than demanding it.

Installing the spare tire, he resolved never to lose his temper in front of someone he wanted. It worked much better to use those innate charms of his to achieve his goals.

* * * *

Jamie Lee sauntered through the crowd into Charley's Rodeo Bar as if he owned the world then sat at the bar next to his best friend, Tommy Parkson. Tommy was one of the few acquaintances he'd yet to alienate.

He slapped Tommy on the back. "Hey Tommy, how's it shaking?"

Tommy turned and stared at him. "Hey Jamie Lee, didn't think I'd see you around tonight. Not with you taking out that babe, Cheryl Alpern. Did you get anywhere? I hear she's a virgin. Is she?"

Jamie Lee could feel the surprise register on his face. "I don't know. She wouldn't screw. Now, I know why." He flashed a mischievous grin. "She did suck me off, though."

Tommy's eyes grew wider. "Is she any good?"

The bartender ambled up in front of him. "What'll ya have Jamie Lee?"

Jamie Lee glanced at the bartender. "Just a draft tonight, Bert."

"So how was it?" Tommy insisted.

The Televangelist I

He grabbed a pretzel and nibbled on it. "I've had better, that's for sure. Inexperienced, I guess. She did manage to get me off though. Came in her mouth. She loved it. Went south with the load, too."

Tommy smiled. "Really, man that must have been so cool, coming in the mouth of someone so pretty. You gonna take her out again?"

Bert set the beer down. "That'll be two-fifty."

Jamie Lee handed him three bucks. "Keep it."

Bert nodded.

Jamie Lee picked up his lager and rotated his bar stool. Looking through the smoky haze, his gaze zeroed in on a cute blonde girl in the booth on the other side of the bar. She wore her hair up with curls draped over a pink ribbon. She sat with three others, a girl and two men all wearing western clothes. Unabashed, Jamie Lee stared at the lady. *She is delicious.* She glanced up and when he caught her gaze, she quickly averted her eyes.

After whispering something to her companion, he nodded and slid out of the booth. She scooted out and headed in the direction of the restrooms, which were opposite of where they sat.

While she glided in their direction, Jamie Lee studied her. She was average in height with blue eyes. She wore a short tight jean skirt, which accentuated the positives and cowboy boots. The creamy skin of her midriff laid exposed, her full breasts covered by a tied off, floral blouse. *I've gotta taste that luscious morsel.*

She must have noticed Jamie Lee staring at her, because she seemed to hold back a smile and several feet from the restroom, her graceful glide turned into a sexy sashay.

Jamie Lee elbowed Tommy and hitched his chin in the direction of the approaching blonde. "Who's the blonde bombshell?"

Tommy followed his stare. "Somebody told me she's Sonny Riverton's daughter. They're in town you know. For a tent revival. You nevah answered me, Bud. You gonna take her out again?"

Staring at the hot blonde, he asked, "Take who out?"

Tommy rolled his eyes. "Cheryl."

"Naw, she's too inexperienced. Now, I'll bet that sweet little thing over there isn't inexperienced. Who's Sonny Riverton, anyway?"

"You never heard of Reverend Riverton? He's on the TV every Sunday." Tommy bit down on a pretzel. "So you wouldn't mind if I asked her out?"

Jamie Lee took a big swig of his beer. "And that's his daughter?"

Tommy slammed his empty beer glass down on the bar. "Damn it, Jamie Lee!"

He turned to Tommy. "What?"

Tommy's gaze rose to the ceiling as if looking for help from a higher power. "Do you care if I ask Cheryl out?"

He did care. Had unfinished business, but when the Reverend's daughter peered at him with that twinkle in her eye and offered a friendly smile, just before turning into the restroom vestibule, he completely forgot about Cheryl.

He shook his head. "Naw. You go ahead. But after tonight, I'd make sure she gargles with Listerine before I kiss her." He punched Tommy lightly on the shoulder and chuckled. "Now, tell me about this tent revival."

"I don't know about this one, but they had another one here two summers ago. The TV station I sometimes work for sent me to film it, which was fine with me, seeing as how I wanted to find out what it was like. Don't you remember it?"

"Naw, musta missed it. Oh, wait, now I remember. I worked as a camp counselor that summer. That's when Maryann Ralencocher and I had that big fling going on every night until we got caught. God, she liked to fuck."

"Jesus, Jamie Lee. I didn't know you were tapping that sweet little thing. I had a big crush on her."

Jamie Lee Vincent shrugged and stuck his hands out to the side as if to say, *when you got it, you got it.* "Go on. Tell me more about this tent revival."

He slid his stool over closer to Jamie Lee. "I gotta tell ya, it was an experience. The preacher was Ray Coombs—Reverend Ray Coombs. There musta been clos'en thousand town folk there. Dey was crying, en faintin,' en prayin' and givin' all their hard earned money to the pastor."

Jamie Lee's eyes thinned to slits. "Really? Why?"

He shrugged and shook his head. "I don't know, I guess, to do God's work and assure their place in heaven. Dat's what the pastor said."

Jamie Lee kept an eye on the restroom entrance. His diligence was rewarded when, after a long minute, she exited. Instead of returning the way she'd come, she headed right, next to the corner between the entrance and the bar where the jute box stood. Jamie Lee's gaze never faltered while she stood in front of the music machine and began swaying her fine little ass to the slow sexy rhythm. *Phew! There ought to be a law.*

Jamie Lee shifted his stiffening manhood. His mind forming carnal thoughts of the two of them in a bed, entwined.

The reverend's cute, blonde daughter turned and swayed in rhythm, up his aisle, to the erotic beat of Bob Segar's, *Turn the Page.*

When she neared, it was do or die, he had to say something. Strolling by, she peeked up demurely and smiled. In a second, she slipped past him. Jamie Lee half yelled, "Hey."

She spun around, an expectant look upon her pretty face. "Me?"

He nodded then blurted out, "You seem to like that song. Would you like to dance?"

The reverend's daughter flashed perfect pearly white teeth when the corners of her mouth curled into a broad smile. "Why yes. I'd love to."

Jamie Lee slid off the stool, took her soft hand, and led her to the dance floor. Jamie Lee's tool stayed rigid and the song being slow and sexy made it worse. Dancing close to this hot lady, there seemed no way he could hide it, nor did he want to. He wanted her to know that he was hot for her, so he pushed his hardness into her softness.

The Televangelist I

Initially, she didn't respond, but after a few thrusts, she pushed back, slightly. *Oh yeah.*

He took his left hand away from hers and looped it around her, joining his right hand on her sweet backside. He squeezed and pushed himself into her again. She pushed back harder and moved her now free hand around his neck, pulling his lips down to her lips. They pecked, and then kissed.

Nice sized breasts pushed into his chest. His tongue slipped past her teeth and entered her mouth.

Was that a sigh? A moan he heard?

They'd stopped dancing. Instead, they swayed to the sexy rhythm of the music and their lusty need.

When the song ended, she broke the kiss and stepped away. "Thank you. That was quite an experience."

"One more?" he pleaded.

"I'm afraid not. I'm much too attracted to you."

Jamie Lee knew she wanted him and felt frustrated. *Don't get angry. Remember, charm.* "That doesn't make sense."

The next song, a fast one started. He cast his most winsome smile. "This is a fast one. C'mon it'll give us a chance to cool down."

She shook her head so hard her ribbon came loose. She pulled out the ribbon and let her hair fall well past her shoulders. "You're much too good looking. Dancing with you makes me want to do improper things. Sorry."

Dumbstruck, he watched as she turned and dashed back to her companions.

The Televangelist I

Twice in one night, a girl denied Jamie Lee. When he rejoined Tommy, thinking about what happened made him grow madder. He wondered if it was too late to visit his old standby, Glenda. *Why not?*

Jamie Lee thought about leaving, when he glanced once more in the direction of the hot blonde. She studied him.

After averting her gaze, she whispered something in her companion's ear. Then to his surprise, the guy looked straight at him and waved him over.

He leaned over and whispered to Tommy, "I'll be right back." He slid off his stool without waiting for a reply and headed toward their booth. The guy who waved him over smiled, stood up, and held out his right hand. He stood tall and had dark hair.

"Hi, I'm Michael Riverton." The blonde kept eyeing him, but didn't say anything. "We're here with the Riverton Big Tent Revival. Did you happen to make the revival tonight?"

He shifted his gaze back and forth between him and her. "Jamie Lee Vincent. No, sorry, I missed it. Had a date."

"I'll bet," the blonde said.

"Well, Missy here—she's my younger sister—she bet me five dollars, you need saving. Now tell me straight, man. Are you a sinner?"

Jamie Lee raised a solitary brow. "Aren't we all?"

"Good point." The blonde said, holding out her hand. Jamie Lee grasped it, but didn't shake it. "Missy Riverton. This is our sister Bobbi Sue and her husband Grant."

The Televangelist I

They nodded and Jamie Lee nodded back. "Charmed, I'm sure."

"What my brother was slowly getting around to is, I'd like to give you a personal invitation to come to the revival and be saved. How 'bout it?"

Jamie Lee bent down and kissed the back of her hand. "Will you be there?"

She nodded. "Oh yes, I'm a channeler. I'll be on stage helping people experience God's forgiveness and feel his grace."

Jamie Lee's head cocked to the side. "If you will personally save me, I'll come."

Her face brightened a hundred watts. "I can do that. Here's my card. Hand it to the security guard tomorrow." She winked. "You don't have a date tomorrow do you?"

Jamie Lee's seductive smile emerged. "Only you, sweet Missy."

She nudged Michael. "Oh, isn't he charming? I have a feeling I'm going to have a lot of fun saving you."

She looked at her brother, then her sister. "You guys ready?"

Michael and Missy slid out of the booth on one side, while Bobbi Sue and Grant slid out on the other. Easing up to Jamie Lee, Missy stood on her tiptoes and kissed him on the cheek. "See you tomorrow."

Jamie Lee could only nod.

"And if you need to talk sooner, my phone number is on my card."

He flicked the card and smiled. *Hot damn and hallelujah.*

* * * *

"Hello."

"It's me…Jamie Lee."

"Hi Jamie Lee. Couldn't wait, huh?"

"Heck no. I want to get to know you. Where're you from, how much longer you're going to be here, if you're involved with anyone. You know, the basics."

Missy giggled. "You're funny. I'm…we're all from Dallas. We have a sticks and bricks House of God there and we shoot a weekly TV sermon. Let's see…we only have four revivals left. Two tomorrow, one Monday and one on Tuesday, so we'll be leaving for Kilgore/Longview Wednesday morning, where we'll have three more revivals before our last stop in Shreveport. What's the other thing you asked? Oh yeah. Am I involved? I am, but not irrevocably."

Without thinking Jamie Lee asked, "Are you intimate?"

"Well, that's an intrusive question. My father is a preacher and I'm a God fearing woman. What do you think?"

"Yes."

"Yes, what?"

She is. I know she is and she wants to fuck me. "You have sex with who you're involved with."

"Well, if I do, it's none of your business."

"Where are you?"

More giggles. "You sure are inquisitive."

"I find you very interesting. Are you in bed?"

The Televangelist I

"Yes."

"Alone?"

"What do you think?"

I wonder. "Are you naked? I'll bet you look fantastic naked."

"No! I'm wearing a nightshirt."

"Pink?"

"Yes, how'd you know?"

"Lucky guess. Are you wearing panties?"

"Are you trying to have phone sex with me?" He was breathing hard. "Jamie Lee, are you masturbating?"

She's a smart one. "Would it bother you if I were?"

"No, but I'm not going to play your silly game. Good night Jamie Lee. See you tomorrow in God's house. Come to the afternoon event."

Chapter Two – Saved
Feminism encourages women to leave their husbands,
kill their children, practice witchcraft, destroy capitalism and
become lesbians. Rev. Pat Robertson

Jamie Lee felt uncomfortable going by himself, so he convinced Tommy to accompanying him. Waiting for Tommy to pick him up, he grew impatient and called him.

"Hello."

"Tommy, Where are you? We need to be there in twenty-five minutes."

"Stop worryin'. I'm only five minutes away en the revival is only a few miles further."

"Tell ya what. We're gonna need to take two cars anyway since Missy said something about saving me personally. I may stay over."

"Yeah right, you're just gonna try to get into her panties."

"That, too. I'll just meet you in front of the entrance."

When Tommy arrived, Jamie Lee already waited in front of the huge tent. The grounds were busy as a state fair. They got in one of the lines to the ticket takers. When they were next in line, Missy's brother,

Michael came over to them and said, "It's okay, Sister Evelyn, I'll take care of these two sinners."

Michael held out his hand.

As Jamie Lee shook it, Tommy questioned, "Sinners?"

Michael glanced at Tommy. "Everyone's a sinner — even my father. We do the best we can.

Michael smiled. "Glad you could make it, Jamie Lee. Missy asked me to see that you were seated and to take care of your comfort. I thought you'd be alone. We'll have to find another seat for your friend here."

He looked back to Tommy, held out his hand and smiled widely. "Hi, I'm Michael Riverton, Reverend Riverton's son. Glad you could join us. Have you found salvation through God?"

Tommy beamed. He shook Michael's hand and replied, "My pleasure. Tommy Parkson. I sure hope so, but you nevah know until the big day comes, do ya?"

Michael winked. "That's why it's a good idea to get saved more than once, Tommy. There's no limit to the number of times you can accept God's grace. Follow me, fellas. We have some special seating set up for our VIPs."

Jamie Lee and Tommy looked at each other, lifted their eyebrows, and followed Michael into the huge tent and right up onto the stage. There were three concentric rows of cushioned folding chairs on the left side of the stage. Already seated were about a dozen people, of whom Jamie Lee recognized only two. City Councilman Ronaldo Aldred, and old Doc Taylor, who was Jamie Lee's pediatrician in his younger days.

The Televangelist I

Michael led them to the back row of the VIP section. "Wait here a minute while I locate another chair." When Michael left them, he stepped over to a burly man with long gray-brown hair in a ponytail and several tattoos on his forearms. The man turned and left the stage while Michael returned.

"I'm sorry. I sent Bill after another chair. We have these things choreographed to the tee and something unexpected can throw us. Since everyone isn't here yet, go ahead and take a seat. When Bill brings the chair just slide over."

They sat down. "Can I get you some refreshments?" asked Michael.

Tommy said, "Nothing for me, thanks."

"Do you have beer?"

"I'm afraid not. We're a progressive church, but not that progressive. I'm afraid I can only offer you coffee, tea, water and Seven-Up." Michael placed his right hand beside his mouth as if he were telling a secret. "The church has stock in Seven-Up."

Jamie Lee shook his head. "I guess I'll pass for now. Thanks for asking."

After Michael left, Jamie Lee glanced around. The tent appeared to be half full and filling fast. Everyone seemed to be ready to have a good time, smiling and shaking the hands of those around them.

When most of the seats were occupied and only stragglers were left to filter in, he saw Cheryl. A surge of white-hot anger flashed through him. *The prissy bitch. I ought to go down there and wring her skinny neck.*

The Televangelist I

Then before he could act upon his rage, the lights dimmed. Their host, Michael Riverton came out wearing what had to be a thousand dollar western tailored suit. When the band started playing, everyone started clapping. One by one, those capable stood, applauding the progeny of the reverend, who waved and bowed as if he'd done something spectacular.

Jamie Lee was in awe of the enthusiasm of the crowd. After a minute, the applause subsided and Michael spoke. "Thank you, thank you very much, I can tell we're going to have a rip-snortin' happening tonight. In all honesty, I must admit you are clapping for the wrong person. I'm Michael Riverton, the reverend's son, merely on stage to introduce God's messenger, Reverend Sonny Riverton." A smattering of clapping started again. "Therefore, without further adieu, here is the great one, my beloved father and mentor, the honorable Reverend Sonny Riverton."

Applause erupted even louder than before. The room grew dark and a solitary spotlight flashed to a side entrance of the tent. There stood a man, probably in his mid fifties in a flashy blue sequined suit and a silver-haired pompadour, waving to the boisterous crowd. When he advanced toward the stage, waving in every direction to those craning their necks, the band cranked out *"Onward Christian Soldiers."*

At the back of the four-foot-high stage, rested a stage set replica of Jesus' head and shoulders. When he reached the stage, the reverend disappeared behind the set. There must have been some stairs and a door through the set, because a few seconds later he emerged through a mist that formed in front of Jesus.

From there he went to Michael, put his arm around him, and took the mic. He waved his hand as if he wanted the lively adoration to end and maybe he did when he attempted to speak over the ruckus. Finally, the crowd quieted. In a deep melodic baritone voice, he said. "Thank you, Thank you very much, Ty-y-y-ler-r-r, Texas." A smattering of applause broke out but quickly subsided. "I love Tyler. Sorry, we haven't been here for awhile, but we've been so busy with the TV show we haven't had time to tour. But now, we have time and here we are in Ty-y-y-ler-r-r, Texas, and I feel blessed to be back."

"Now, let me ask you, how many of you God lovin', God fearin' folks watch our TV show, Soldiers of the Lord?" The reverend stifled the clapping with a stern hand. "No folks. I want to see hands; and remember, God will know if you lie."

About twenty percent of the hands went up.

"Fair enough. It's my own fault for not being here for a while. But I swear to you, the Big Tent of the Lord will be back every year or my name isn't Sonne-e-e-e-e!"

After a short standing ovation, he continued. "Now, those that watch 'The Soldiers of the Lord,' and those that came four years ago when we were last here, know that I don't usually quote scripture—chapter and verse. Honestly, for almost every verse that says one thing, I could quote another verse that seems to contradict it. No, what I do is explain what God

The Televangelist I

expects from us, his humble servants. For starters, God expects us to be moral creatures. By that, I mean...

The reverend spoke for about fifteen minutes, explaining what God wants of his flock. After that, he introduced a man who sang, *'You gave me a Mountain.'* Next, he introduced a woman who soloed, *'Ave Maria.'* Then together they sang a duet of *'Peace in the Valley.'* Afterward a choir joined them for a grand performance of *'The Battle Hymn of the Republic,'* which brought a rousing round of applause from the audience.

The entertainment continued in the form of exhibitions. A group of four put on a tumbling exercise and a man displayed his dexterity by maintaining spinning plates on up to ten separate poles.

Jamie Lee was getting bored, until the reverend came back out for the remaining portion of his address. This was the part Jamie Lee wanted to see most—the passing of the collection plates. "The first thing our Lord expects from us is generosity. Generosity to those less fortunate than us, the sick, the infirm, the poor, the hopeless. Donations to 'Soldiers of the Lord' help all of these unfortunate souls. However, most of all, God cherishes money given freely to him, in care of our ministry. Dig deep. Deep as you can. Until it hurts, for God loves and helps those that hurt. For those that have special requests, a notepad is attached to the collection plate. Write your request then place it in the collection plate. Those that need healing, write your name and what needs healing. Our volunteers will pass a plate by all of you. When they finish, we are going to save some souls and perform some healing. Are you ready for that?"

The audience replied with a modicum of yeses and amens.

"What? I didn't hear you. Are you ready for that?"

The audience exploded in affirmation and the reverend smiled.

"That was good. I heard you that time. Now, it's time to introduce you to my lovely daughters, Missy and Bobbi Sue. They are my channelers. God works his magic through them. Let's hear a big hand for Missy and Bobbie Sue."

The throng rose, then, clapped for a good minute when the two ladies, dressed in white dresses and heels with a white ribbon in their hair, entered the stage the same way Sonny did. Mixed in with the applause this time were whistles and catcalls, which prompted the reverend to calm them down.

Missy glanced over to Jamie Lee and cast a broad, white smile just before her father signaled to the band conductor to start. They started with the old Dionne Warwick song, 'What the World Needs Now is Love.' Then the choir joined in. The band played four songs while some dozen or more ushers passed the collection plates.

They orchestrated everything to raise money. Jamie Lee's heart thumped in his chest from excitement. The audience handed over their money as if their life depended on it. Maybe they believed it did. The guy sitting next to him put a hundred dollar bill in the plate. When they handed the plate to him he quickly tried to assess the haul as he deposited his dollar — six or seven hundred dollars from twenty- four people. If they raised even a third of that from the rest of the audience, it would add up to almost ten thousand dollars. Not a bad haul for a Sunday morning.

Jamie Lee nudged his friend. "Man, I gotta get into this racket. Look at them raking in the dough."

Tommy, who seemed caught up in the minute, turned to Jamie Lee with a tight-lipped frown. "I thought ya didn't believe in God?"

"I believe in the green God — money!"

Tommy's eyes thinned. "How cynical."

"Hey, I'm a realist."

After passing the collection plates, one of the ushers brought up a bowl with all the slips from the audience and handed it to Reverend Riverton. He pulled a slip and called the name, "Janette Carlson. Come up so God can heal you, through us, his servants."

An attractive matronly, middle-aged woman stood up. Focusing on no one, she yelled, "That's me," She walked slowly, if judiciously toward the stage. An usher helped her up the stage and she carefully walked to the three Rivertons. The reverend divulged that she suffered from chronic advanced diabetes causing her vision to deteriorate.

The audience seemed mesmerized. You could hear a pin drop as the reverend led Ms. Carlson to a chair, where he gently helped her to sit. Each of the sisters took one of her arms with one of their hands and put their other arm around dad, who crowded in close.

The reverend and lady's conversation was inaudible to Jamie Lee and likely everyone else, too, since he sat in the closest group. Sonny placed his hands on the lady's head just below her ears and appeared to be speaking to her earnestly. Then he placed one hand behind her head and the other on her forehead. He looked skyward and yelled, "Lord Jesus, I beg of you. Look down upon thy servant, Janette Carlson and heal her — make her whole again. After pushing on her forehead, he stepped back as if Jesus had said something to him and said, "Thank you, Lord."

Ms Carlson shook her head like snapping out of a trance, and cried, "My God, I can see. She hugged the reverend, wildly. "Thank you. I don't know how to thank you properly. You saved my life."

The reverend adamantly shook his head. "Not so. We were merely the vehicles. Our Lord Jesus is the one who healed you. Now you must pay him back with your love."

Ms Carlson embraced each of the sisters, saying in between, "Oh, I do. I love God more than life. Thank you, God."

On cue, the audience let it rip. The largest and longest sustained applause yet, and while everyone still clapped, she exited the platform with a vitality that wasn't evident on her trip to the stage.

The Televangelist I

The cycle repeated. Call a name, someone would stand or jump up if able, acting like the winners of the Publisher's Clearing House Contest. They came up on the stage and, with varied techniques from the agents of God, were cured of whatever ailed them.

The audience, apparently transfixed because of the healings, fascinated Jamie Lee. *I can do this!*

After the seventeenth and last healing, the reverend invited everyone to line up for salvation. Tommy and Jamie Lee rose, but Missy shook her head at Jamie Lee and mouthed. *No.* When Jamie Lee hesitated, Tommy asked, "You coming?"

"Go ahead. Missy wants me to wait."

Tommy nodded and hurried to get in line.

The routine went generally the same. The lucky person whose turn it was to be saved went up on the stage and stood in a circle. The reverend stepped in front of the initiate with a bucket of water into which the person stuck both hands. When they withdrew their hands, they would rub their face with their wet hands. Missy, who stood beside the Godly recruit, holding an arm, presented a towel for them to dry off. Bobbi Sue, on the other side, took the used towel and put it in a basket. Then, like he did on the initial healing, the reverend placed a hand behind the novitiate's head and while reciting something, pushed on his or her forehead with his fingers. Some of the newcomers fell backward into the waiting arms of Michael.

Jamie Lee decided to count the new followers and on the forty-sixth devotee, a flash of heat coursed through him. His heart skipped a beat as the bitch—Cheryl—came up. *What the fuck does she need saving for? She's a virgin. Probably coveting my dick.* Jamie Lee released an evil chuckle.

There were only six more proselytes after Cheryl. The revival closed with '*Amazing Grace*' and everyone seemed exhilarated when they exited.

Jamie Lee turned to Tommy who'd returned to his seat after the ceremony. "So what did the reverend say when he saved you?"

"He said somethin' like, dear Lord Jesus, Please accept the sinner Thomas Parkson as your humble servant en forgive—"

"You ready, hot stuff?" Jamie Lee felt a tug on his sleeve. They both looked up at Missy, whose bright, white smile lit up the tent.

Jamie Lee stood and splayed his hands to his side. "Gotta go, bro. Duty calls. We'll finish what we were talking about later. All right?"

"Sure, no problem. I saw Cheryl here. I think I'll see if I can find her."

Jamie Lee didn't like that one bit, but with Missy tugging on his arm there wasn't much he could do.

The Televangelist I

Chapter Three – Salvation

I believe that all of us are born heterosexual, physically
created with a plumbing that's heterosexual.
Rev. Jerry Falwell

Jamie Lee put his arm around Missy. "Where're we going, cupcake?"

She started walking toward the side stage stairs. "We're headed to the sanctuary."

"I thought this was the sanctuary."

When they reached the stairs, she took Jamie Lee's hand and led him down the stairs. "This is God's sanctuary. We're going to my sanctuary. My motor home."

He smiled as visions of the two of them entwined in a bed, returned.

Missy pulled the tent flap back enough to slip through sideways and dragged Jamie Lee behind her. To his surprise, it had started to get dark, which meant the revival had lasted over three hours. She made a right turn and followed the edge of the tent to the corner then stopped. "Well, what'dya think?"

Jamie Lee came up behind her, put his free arm around her waist, and snuggled his head against her neck. "About what?" he whispered.

"Good golly, didn't God give you eyes? Mmmm, you're getting fresh, but it feels good."

Jamie Lee looked around the corner. There sat a huge motor home, with Missy written on the side in large silver letters on a pink background. "Wow, that's where you live?"

"Ah huh. But only when we tour." She turned around and faced Jamie Lee. "Now, I can tell from the look in your eyes that you think you're going to make love to me. I suppose a hunk like you is used to getting his way, but we need to get things straight between us and I don't mean your penis. I can tell you are bad for me, but I can't resist those sad brown eyes and that sideways smile. I still have a boyfriend, so we are not...I repeat, *not* going to make love. You got that straight?"

"I guess, but what are we going to do?"

"Well for starters I'm gonna save your ass and I'll wager your tight little buns need a lot of saving. Am I right?"

Jamie Lee felt a flush of warmth course through him, but he didn't answer.

Missy unlocked the front door and stepped into the mammoth vehicle. Jamie Lee followed. "Wow! This is something else. What kind of motor home is it?"

"It's called a Zephyr. Its forty feet long and costs more than the average house."

"Man, this is luxurious. Do you drive it?"

The Televangelist I

"Heavens, no. Daddy has someone drive it for me."

Missy took Jamie Lee's hand again and dragged him to a built-in sofa. She sat down and pulled him down next to her. She tucked one leg under the other in such a way that she almost turned toward him.

He looked at her. "I'd like to be your driver."

She twined her fingers on Jamie Lee's shoulder. "Would you now?"

"You bet, and when I'm not driving I could help set up. Do you think your daddy would hire me?"

Missy leaned in closer. "He might, if I batted my lashes at him." She closed her eyes, while moving her lips toward his. She sighed when their lips touched. She parted her lips slightly, inviting his tongue to join hers. He could feel her hands tensing on his shoulder when he slid his tongue through the small opening between her teeth and touched hers.

Slowly, she pulled away. "Mmm, that was nice. I'd better get you saved before you have another sin to excise. I have a feeling you're a real bad boy, aren't you?"

Jamie Lee laughed. "I never thought so. I just like to have fun and feel good." He put his hand on her breast. "I'll bet you could make me feel real good."

She took the offending hand and held it. "And I know you could make me feel good too, but alas, it's not going to happen...tonight."

Jamie Lee's head tilted to the side and he looked at her expectantly. "Tomorrow?"

The Televangelist I

She lifted his hand to her lips and kissed it. "As much as I'd like too, I'm afraid not."

Now, he frowned. "When?"

She sighed. "Hon, I want you too. Really I do. I can almost feel your hardness inside me, but first I need a commitment and then I have the boyfriend to dispose of. He's not someone to take lightly."

A pinch of anger assaulted him. "Who is he?"

"Sweetie, you don't need to know that. Now, let's get those clothes off so I can save you."

Jamie Lee's brows furrowed as he imparted a sideways gaze. "Take my clothes off? What're you talking about?"

She giggled. "I'm going to wash away your sins in holy water. Just like a baptism. And I might add, I'm looking forward to it."

"But all the others just stuck their hands in a pail of water."

"That's because we're on the road. Back home in Dallas we would have immersed them all in water. Course, unlike you, they'd have the option of wearing a bathing suit." She stood and with two hands pulled him to his feet. "Let's get you started." She led him to the good-sized bedroom in the back of the bus. "Take all your clothes off." She opened the door to the bathroom. "Then get in that tub. I'm going to make arrangements for some holy water to be brought here."

Standing legs apart, she bent her elbows and rested her fists akimbo on her hips. "Well."

"Well, what?"

The Televangelist I

She hitched her pretty chin at him. "Get started, baby."

After flashing what was supposed to be a look of disgust, a smile replaced it. He unbuttoned his shirt and removed his shirt. "Always figured I'd make a good stripper."

Mmm. You would make a good stripper. "Love those ripples in your tummy."

"You gonna stay for the whole show?"

"No, Babe." She stood on her toes and kissed his cheek. "I'll see the whole show when I get back."

* * * *

She left the motor home and headed for the water truck, which contained two thousand gallons of holy water. She ran into Bill and asked him to come with her. When they reached the water truck and referring to the five-gallon bottles, she asked him, "Can you carry two bottles if I carry one?"

"I think I can carry three."

"Good fill them up. Hand the first one to me and bring the rest to my motor home."

"Yes ma'am."

With the first bottle in hand, she entered the bathroom. He stood there naked except for a towel around his waist. "Don't you knock?"

"You're a big boy." Looking him up and down, she couldn't see a flaw on him. He looked magnificent. She shook off the idea that maybe she should make love to him and stared at the makeshift loincloth. "What's with the towel? You shy or something?"

The Televangelist I

He turned a little red and the right side of his lips turned upward into the sideways smile she'd seen before. "It doesn't seem right for me to be totally naked lessen' we're going to do something."

She walked past him and poured the water into the tub. "I have three more bottles comin'. Since you want to screw me so bad, you shouldn't mind me seein' your weezer. Unless it's laughable."

"Missy, I guarantee it ain't."

"Good. Then lose the towel and get in." She was afraid the improper urges she had might overwhelm her and cloud her judgment, so she turned and left before she had a chance to do either.

While she headed to the kitchen, Bill brought the other three bottles of holy water in. "Where do you want these, Missy?"

"Just leave them there. I can handle them from there one at a time. Thanks."

He raised his hand to his forehead in a mock salute. "Anytime."

She continued into the kitchen and scrounged for a large ladle. You'd think with her connection with God, she'd be able to find things easier, but as usual, she found what she looked for in the last possible spot.

She shoved the ladle in her dress' belt, picked up one of the bottles and headed into the bathroom. She set the bottle down, pulled the cap off, and lifted the bottle to the edge of the tub where it slowly poured into the reservoir. His cock looked stiff as a board and aimed toward the heavens. "Have you been playin' with yourself?"

The Televangelist I

He raised his hands in mock surrender. "No, ma'am, I was just thinking about you. You reckon God is trying to tell us something."

Lord help me. His oversized manhood drew her gaze like a magnet. "I doubt it. You're either a horny toad or you were whacking off. Now, I have two more bottles to pour in here so keep your hands off your equipment."

After she'd finished pouring the holy water she pulled the ladle from her belt, got on her knees, and whispered, "What's your full name?"

"Jamie Lee Vincent."

"Dear Lord Jesus." She scooped the ladle full of water and poured it over his head. "We have with us Jamie Lee Vincent." She poured more water over him. "Please accept this repentant sinner for your humble servant," She poured more water. "And forgive his numerous trespasses, before thee."

"Are you done?"

She shook her head. "Not yet, I have to dunk you." She placed her left hand at the back of his head, while her right put pressure on his chest to lay back. He lay back, submerging his face.

He rose up. "Am I saved now?"

She nodded. "Ah-huh." Then before she knew what happened, he grabbed her arms and jerked her into the tub, dress, shoes and all.

She rose up on her hands. "What'd you do that for? You ruined my dress," she cried.

The fire of desire inhabited his eyes as he stared at her. With water running down his slender frame Jamie

Lee stood, naked yet unashamed. Hauling her to her feet, his bare maleness unrestrained, pressed against her abdomen. His lips crushed hers in a bruising kiss, while his hands removed her sopping wet dress. While her clothes came off, his intuitive fingers courted her breasts and vulva, know exactly what to do for maximum effect. A sensual cloud passed over her and she reacted, not indignantly, like she should have, but instinctively, kissing him back in a frenzied display of passion and stroking his silky hardness. Falling into a vortex of lust, she lost control. To her shame, they made love...until the wee hours.

* * * *

Searching for her car in the parking lot after the revival broke up she heard her name called. "Hi, Cheryl."

She turned. It was Tommy Parkson, that asshole Jamie Lee's friend. Unlike Jamie Lee, he was nice — good-looking, too. Why he hung with Jamie Lee, she'd never know. She smiled and paused to let him catch up. "Hi, Tommy. It looks like we have something in common, now."

His eyes grew wide. "We do?"

To his surprise, she took his arm as they started walking again. "Yep. We both belong to the Lord now."

He smiled broadly. "We do, don't we, en to celebrate, I'd like to take ya to Baskin en Robbins for a treat. Would ya like dat?"

"I'd love it." She kissed his cheek and peeled away toward her car. "See you there."

The Televangelist I

Tommy, number in hand, waited for service when she arrived. It looked like half the people at the revival had the same idea. There must have been fifty people there. She sidled up to Tommy and wrapped her arm around his upper arm. "Hi."

He smiled, pulled his arm away from her hand, and looped it around her. She liked the way it felt.

"What would ya like?"

She placed her forefinger to her lips while she thought. "Ahhh...can I get a double?"

"You can have anythin' your little heart desires. After all, it's like a birthday. You were born again."

She always liked Tommy and knew he had eyes for her, but he never did anything. "Well, since it's like my birthday, I'll have a hot fudge sundae."

"You got it. Why don't ya see if you can scrounge a table while I wait for number G77?"

She laughed and kissed him on the cheek again. When she turned to look for a table, a couple and their two young children got up. She rushed over, staking her claim. "Are you leaving?"

The woman said, "Yes, we are. It's all yours."

She sat at the back of the table so she could watch Tommy. When he saw her, he flashed a thumb up. She batted her eyelashes and he chuckled. *Today is turning out to be a pretty good day.*

Finally, after a twenty minute wait her sundae and makeshift date sat in front of her. When she dug in with her plastic spoon, she felt a pang of longing as Tommy licked what looked like a chocolate chip ice

The Televangelist I

cream cone. She crossed one leg over the other. "So what did you think?"

"'Bout the revival? I thought da put on a pretty good show. You know, entertainin'. I'm just not so sure of some of the tings dat happened. You know what I mean?"

"Sure, I know what you mean, but if you felt like that, why'd you get saved?"

He fidgeted in his seat. "Well, I kind of got stuck, up there on the stage with Jamie Lee."

Her head shook. "Yeah, I saw that. Talk about the fox in the chicken coop."

Tommy's brows furrowed. "What'd ya mean by that?"

She shrugged. "Nothing. How come Jaime Lee didn't get saved?"

"Oh, he was Missy Riverton's guest. She's gonna save him herself."

She felt her eyes widen. "That bubbly, cute, little girl — the reverend's daughter?"

"Uh-huh."

Her gaze shifted to the ceiling, while she absorbed that. "I hope she knows what she's doing."

His brow dipped. "Why?"

"Let's just say he's not the nicest person on the planet."

He took her left hand and smiled. "Well, the good thing is wit' him seeing Missy, I can see you."

She smiled. "That is good, but Tommy, I didn't belong to Jamie Lee. You coulda asked me out anytime you wanted."

The Televangelist I

He looked conflicted. His nostrils flared and his pretty blue-eyed gaze bored into her. "You know how it is wit friends. Once someone says they're interested in someone, ya back off en give dem a chance. If it don't work out, ya get your chance, den."

She swallowed her last spoonful of fudge sundae and put her other hand over their two. "Believe me, Jamie Lee never had a chance, but you do, so what're you going to do about it?"

He wiggled and fidgeted again. Averting his gaze, he asked, "Would you like ta go to dinner en a movie this weekend?"

Chapter Four – Tommy and Cheryl
I respect the agnostic who has serious questions -- but the atheist is an emotional deviate. That's caused to a great degree by getting out of our natural habitat.
Rev. Robert H. Schuller

After a frenzied night of lovemaking, Missy should have woken in a state of beatitude. Instead, she felt bitterly disappointed in herself. After capturing her imagination, this man, whom she barely knew, seized her heart and she'd succumbed to his wiles. Inexorably, her gaze went to him. He was so handsome, and charming, and mesmerizing that he beguiled her into having sex with him less than twenty-four hours after meeting him.

She'd cheated on her fiancé of two years with a virtual stranger. She hated herself. She hated the weakness of her flesh. This man seemed to be everything she wanted, but intrinsically, she knew he wasn't good for her.

Dear Lord God, It is I, your devoted servant, Missy Riverton. I need your help. Share your powerful strength and wisdom with me. Help me fight off Jamie Lee Vincent's charms. Give me the vision to see into his heart, which I suspect is deceptive. Bestow wisdom upon me so I can make proper judgments. And most of all forgive me for my lapse of Christian morals and fornicating with this man. Thank you, Jesus. I know you won't let me dow – .

* * * *

Opening his eyes, Jamie Lee beheld Missy's gorgeous naked body and beautiful profile. So it wasn't a dream. It seemed almost too good to be true. With her long blonde hair and baby blues, she looked like a real life Barbie Doll and he fucked the hell out of her. *She is, without a doubt, my greatest conquest.*

With closed eyes, she mumbled something. Could it be a prayer? Does she really buy that Jesus crap her daddy spouts? Immaculate conception, resurrection, burn in hell. Only the gullible, brainwashed and feeble-minded could truly believe. How many so-called believers pretended to believe, for economical or social reasons? Millions and millions he'd bet. Hypocrites!

He wondered what she prayed for. He snickered mentally. Probably praying for him to wake up and fuck her some more. He certainly felt hard enough.

I'm hard and I want me some Missy pussy. He reached over and ran his finger along her clit. She jumped as if she'd received an electric shock. She jumped out of bed and, standing there, naked as a newborn, frowned and wagged a finger at him.

"Don't touch me. Last night didn't happen. Understand?"

He frowned. "Well, if last night didn't happen, how come I'm in your bed, harder than a rock, and you're buck naked?"

The Televangelist I

She set her legs about thirty inches apart and rested her hands on her hips. *God, she looks good.* "You're not listening. Last night should *not* have happened, therefore, it *didn't* happen. It was your imagination. Now, I think you should leave."

This shocked him. He had this girl locked up and now she's ordering him to leave. *Don't lose your temper. Use the charm.* He chuckled, "You know, I'm not proud of it, but I've had a few one night stands. I swear to God, I never thought I would be a one night stand."

Her harsh façade softened a little. "You're not a one night stand."

"No, what am I, a stud on loan? How many climaxes did you have last night? Five?"

"I had six, but since last night didn't happen, I had no climaxes and by extension you couldn't be a one night stand. Beside, you have my phone number and can call me."

"Do you want me to call?"

She nodded vigorously. "Yes, I just need time to think and commune with the Lord about what happened."

He chuckled. "Or what didn't happen."

She snickered. "Good point."

He rose from the bed and his hard cock drew her gaze. He caught her tongue sliding surreptitiously over her upper lip.

"Will I get to see you before you leave on Wednesday?"

"No."

The Televangelist I

She walked up to him. They were both naked and his lust seemed unending. His dick poked her abdomen, but she shoved it aside. "I'm sorry, but I can't trust myself with you, yet. I'll be back in Dallas in a week. It isn't that far. I promise I'll see you then, either here or there. Now, get dressed and outta here before someone sees you. I have to get ready. We'll be heading out shortly for Kilgore."

* * * *

"Hello?"

"Hey Missy, it's Jamie Lee. Did you leave yet?"

"Hi, sweetheart. Yeah, I'm afraid we're almost to Kilgore. Why?"

"I miss you. You left quite an impression on me. I'd hoped to say goodbye before you left."

She didn't respond for about fifteen seconds. "You left an impression on me, too."

"How many revivals are you gonna have there?"

"Two, tomorrow night, and Friday night. Why?"

"Well, hell, I could drive the twenty-five miles up there in no time. I thought I'd come to tomorrow's show and take you out afterward for coffee."

Another pause. "I don't drink coffee."

"Well, iced tea then or a malt. Whatever you want."

"Friday would be better. I've gotta go."

* * * *

"Where are we going?"

Tommy shifted his glance from the road for a second and smiled. "I thought we'd start at El Chicos or da Olive Garden. Are ya in a Mexican or Italian mood?"

"I haven't had Italian in a while. Let's go there."

Ten minutes later, they walked into a very packed Olive Garden. "Twenty minute wait," he told her, "Do ya want ta wait?"

"Sure, by the time we go somewhere else, it'd be twenty minutes. Let's wait outside though."

Tommy added his name to the list and met her outside. He walked up to her. She wrapped her arms around him and laid her cheek on his chest. The strong beat of his heart on his chest wall curled the corners of her lips. He wrapped his arms around her. "I got invited ta a party, tonight, but I figured ya wouldn't want to go."

"Why, is your friend Jamie Lee going to be there?"

"No, because there's going to be drinking. Why, do ya want to see him?"

She rolled her eyes. "Hah! That'll be the day."

"Then why did ya go out wit him?"

She pulled away and looked Tommy in the eye. "Because I didn't know he was such an asshole until I went out with him."

"Well if ya think he's such an asshole, why did'ya…"

"Why did I what?"

"Look, I want ya to know what you did with Jamie Lee doesn't matter to me. I know he has a way with women and if ya have him out of your system, I don't care what ya did with him."

She couldn't believe it. Her head shook in earnest. "No, no, no! You don't get out of it that easy. Did he say he fucked me?"

Now it became Tommy's turn to shake his head. "No, he didn't."

"What then? Suck his cock?"

His mouth fell open and mimicked the size and shape of silver dollars. "Um, er…"

She handed him her phone. "Get that son-of-a-bitch on the phone."

He took it and punched in the number. "Jamie Lee, Cheryl wants to talk with ya."

"I'm on a date with her."

"Yes, you did." I asked you at the Rodeo, en you said it was okay."

"Why not?"

"You're in Kilgore?"

"What're ya doing there?"

"She did? You lucky devil."

"All right. Have fun." He pushed end and handed the phone back to her.

"He wouldn't talk to me huh?"

"No. he said he's busy at another tent revival in Kilgore. He's there to see Missy Riverton again—lucky guy."

"Oh, that poor girl."

"Parkson, party of two."

He took her hand. "That's us."

"Good, I'm starved and after we eat, I think I'd like to go to that party."

He smiled. "All right. I think ya have Jamie Lee wrong. I'm sure he really likes the Riverton daughter."

"He should. She's sweet and beautiful, but I'm afraid the only person Jamie Lee likes is Jamie Lee."

* * * *

"Hello,"

"Missy. It's Jamie Lee. I'm in the audience."

"Go to the side entrance of the tent." He hung up.

God, you never gave me any direction. I hope I'm doing the right thing.

Five minutes after hanging up, her heart seemingly skipped a beat at the sight of him. Her poor stomach clenched as he drew closer. He walked up to her and tried to kiss her. She turned her cheek. "Not here. People will see you. Here's the key to my motor home. Go there and wait for me. Do not, I repeat, do not get undressed. We are only going to talk."

The Televangelist I

Chapter Five – Jamie Lee's Engagement
*And that is why I think that God has used it in churches
because we have seen a lot of healing take place in churches
and we have seen a lot of healing take place in families.*
Rev. Kerry Shook

After letting himself in to Missy's Motor home, Jamie Lee entered the kitchen and opened the refrigerator door on the minimal chance there might be a six-pack of beer in there. There wasn't, so he grabbed a bottle of Dr. Pepper and headed to the couch. After taking a swig of the tangy soda, he picked up the remote, turned on the TV, and switched the channel until he came to Miami Vice. He looked at his watch — seven-oh-five. If this revival went like the one in Tyler, Missy would be walking up the stairs after ten p.m.

After Miami Vice, he switched to Mission Impossible and when that was over, he found a rerun of Charlie's Angels. He liked that. Watching three beautiful women cavorting around put him in a good mood.

Damned if Cheryl Ladd didn't look like Missy. *Remember, use charm on Missy. This girl loves you. Let her reel you in until you get what you want.*

He dozed off around nine-thirty and woke at ten-fifteen when a gentle hand crossed his forehead.

Sitting up on the couch, he rubbed his eyes. Jamie Lee looked for Missy and rubbed his eyes a second time to make sure he wasn't imaging things. Missy's father, Reverend Sonny Riverton sat there, staring at him. He had to admire Missy. She was full of surprises and kept him guessing—always off balance.

The reverend's deep baritone voice boomed out. "Sorry to wake you, son." The man's large paw reached across the coffee table. "I'm Sonny Riverton and Missy is my daughter."

What's going on? Did she tell him about us? Did she tell him I fucked the shit out of her? Is he going to insist we get married?

Missy walked into the room and handed a large cup to Sonny. "Here's your coffee, papa." After Sonny takes the cup Missy asks, "Mr. Vincent would you like some coffee, too?"

If Reverend Riverton could have coffee, so could Mr. Vincent. He smiled at the possible, future Mrs. Vincent. "Please, I would love a cup. Cream only." He shook Sonny's ham of a hand. "Jamie Lee Vincent, sir. It's an honor to meet you."

"Likewise. Now, my little honey tells me you two shared a *very* intimate session."

Jamie Lee's mouth remained open while the reverend took a sip of coffee.

"Where she acted as your personal savior and brought you to Jesus. Is that right?"

"That's right sir and I ju—"

The Televangelist I

Sonny held a hand up. "If you'll be patient and let me finish. You can speak then."

Missy brought a coffee carafe. A cup and creamer on a tray and set it on the table while she sat next to her daddy. She poured coffee in the cup, added cream and handed it to him. "Here you go Mr. Vincent."

"Thank you." He took the cup and a sip while Sonny continued. "As I was saying, Missy claims that after you accepted Jesus as your savior, you indicated a desire to serve God. Is that right Jamie Lee?"

"That's right, sir."

He lifted the cup to his lips once more and set it down. "Good. Now we're getting to the crux of things. Missy also tells me you have amorous inclinations toward her and she to you. You know she is seeing the son of a powerful televangelist in Atlanta. That connection would be an asset to our ministry, but Missy is my favorite and if she prefers you, I'm inclined to let her have her way, on one condition."

As he took another sip of his coffee, Jamie Lee took the opportunity to speak, "What is that, sir?"

The intensity of the reverend's stare began to rattle Jamie Lee when he spoke, "I want to see into your soul. I want to know that your wish to serve God is a calling and not just a job. I want to know that when you marry my daughter, you will love her, respect her, and never lay a hand on her, for if you do, Jamie Lee, you will feel my wrath. Next, I want to hear about your personal experience when Jesus accepted you and I want to hear about the fire in your belly you feel to serve God."

The Televangelist I

Marry Missy? *I certainly entertained the possibility, but this is awful quick.* "In all due respect sir, we never talked about marriage and while your daughter is a prize I would treasure, this is moving along too fast."

Sonny's nostrils flared and he looked annoyed. "You make a good point son. Since you won't tell me about your personal experience when Jesus accepted you, let *me* tell you. Shortly after your personal savior, Missy, brought you to Jesus, you copulated with her in the same holy water that had saved you."

Jamie Lee's stomach turned over. Missy *did* tell him.

"Then you went into your savior's bed and fornicated with her for hours as they surely do in the bowels of Hell. The next morning, when you wanted to continue your fornication, she asked you to leave. Is that about what you experienced?"

What could he say? He nodded.

"Lest you think Missy told me, let me explain. I told Missy what happened. Missy and to a lesser extent her sister are channelers. God wanted you to fuck my daughter. God wants you to be together. That is why I came to speak with you in a reasonable tone instead of having Bill break both your arms and throw you off the lot.

"However, through the years, I have found that God is not infallible and on very rare occasions, makes mistakes. If he was wrong about you, it's not too late and it would give me extreme joy to have Bill forcibly escort you from the premises. Do I make myself clear?"

The Televangelist I

He wants me to marry his daughter. To save her honor. "Yes sir, however, if I may be so bold, I think you are wrong about one thing. While people make mistakes, God doesn't. Since we have no knowledge of his reasons and purposes, we cannot judge his results. He is omnipotent. He is infallible. You're right. God wanted me to fuck your daughter. He wants us to be together and I dare not go against almighty God."

Sonny's face remained solemn for a while and then a broad smile ushered forth. Squeezing hard, he nearly broke Jamie Lee's hand as he shook it. "Spoken like a true revivalist. I see a big future for you." Still holding Jamie Lee's hand, the Reverend lifted him up and embraced him. "Welcome to the family, son."

Missy came over and hugged them as best she could.

After a long hug, Reverend went into the kitchen to get a coffee refill while Missy pulled Jamie Lee's lips down for an engagement kiss. When the kiss lasted about a minute longer than it took Sonny to get his coffee, he said, "Ahem. Now that we have Missy's future figured out, we have to work out some details."

They broke the kiss and the two men sat down while Missy happily fetched her future husband a refill for his coffee cup.

"Here's the way I see it. We will need about two weeks to extricate Missy from her engagement to Donald Robson, son of Pat Robson. After that's accomplished, we'll wait two months to announce her engagement to you.

"Now tell me son. What do you do?"

The Televangelist I

Missy set Jamie Lee's coffee down and took a seat close to him.

Jamie Lee figured he'd marry Missy to get into the Riverton clan's inner circle, but the speed and smoothness with which the Reverend had brought about their engagement threw him. He made a mental note not to underestimate the good reverend in the future. "Ah, I been workin' in a full service gas station. I'm learning to be a mechanic."

"That will never do. How old are you?"

"Almost twenty-four."

"Okay, here's what we'll do. Starting right now, you are working for the 'Soldiers of the Lord.' Prior to that, you attended Hardin Simmons University for the last two semesters via one of our Christian scholarships. Obviously, since you never left Tyler, you took the courses by correspondence." He chuckled. "I always knew those scholarships would come in handy some day."

"Daddy, when would the wedding take place?"

"Well darlin', the wedding will take place five months after we announce your engagement. That would put it sometime in March."

"Ooh, that seems so far off. Would Jamie Lee and I be able to...lay with each other before then?"

"I don't see why not. Just be discreet." He wagged a finger at Jamie Lee. "Don't you dare get my baby knocked up, ya hear?"

* * * *

Missy got a call from her dad the next morning.

The Televangelist I

"Jamie Lee, my dad would like you to meet with him in his motor home."

His gaze shifted up from the Saturday morning cartoon on the TV to her. "What about?"

She shrugged. "I'm not sure. He said something about paperwork."

Jamie Lee watched workmen break down the tent and loading segments of it on an eighteen-wheeler as he strolled to the other side of the back lot—to the reverend's identical Zephyr motor home. "Come in," came the reply to Jamie Lee's tentative knock on the door. He stepped inside and noticed his future father-in-law sitting at a fancy desk busily writing on a tablet. "Have a seat, son. I'll be with you in a minute." Scanning the room, which had been a living room in Missy's motor home, he noticed an attractive redheaded lady typing away at a desk on the far side of the room near the driver's cocoon.

He stepped over and took a seat in one of two chairs that fronted Reverend Riverton's desk. He crossed his left leg over the right, and tapping his fingers on the arm of the chair, he continued to look around. The room was set up like an office on wheels, with computers, a copy machine, and file cabinets. Everything appeared to be the best money could buy.

While Jamie studyed the photos on the wall to his right, the red head suddenly appearing on his left, tapped him on the shoulder. As he turned his head toward her, she flashed a winsome smile. Holding a clipboard in her left hand, she offered her right hand. "Hi, I'm Gwen. Welcome to SOL."

He had to think for a second what that meant and then remembered the ministry called itself 'Soldiers of the Lord.' He shook her hand and studied her. Jamie Lee Vincent. "Pleased to meet you." He was, too. She was very attractive. Red heads had never appealed to him, but this one did. She was exceptional.

Bending down, her low cut blouse afforded a clear view of her shapely breasts as she handed him the clipboard, which had a form and a pen clamped to it. "I need you to fill out this employment application and a W-9 form." With his gaze glued to her impressive rack, he took the clipboard and set it in his lap conveniently covering the sudden swelling taking place below.

Gwen smiled again. "Can I get you something to drink?"

His gaze switched from Gwen's breasts to her eyes. He smiled. "Coffee, if you have it."

She snickered. "Oh, I think I can find some."

As Jamie Lee watched her shapely legs escort her sweet ass to the hallway, he heard the reverend clear his throat. His gaze shifted and he saw Sonny gaping at him over his reading glasses. "You are taken, and so is she."

Properly chastised, he nodded and dutifully filled the application out.

When he finished he handed the clip board to the reverend. "Here you go, sir."

He took it and glanced over it. "You didn't fill in closest living relative, son."

"That'd be my mom, Consuela Vincent."

The reverend's eyes narrowed. "She's Mexican?"

"Half." Jamie Lee fidgeted. "Is that a problem?"

"Not as long as I know about it. What's her address and phone number?"

"1242 West Nautilus Street, Tyler, 903-555-9392."

"You live there, with your mother?"

"Ah-huh."

"Where's your dad?"

He lifted his right leg over his left. "Don't know."

"What'dya mean, you don't know? Is he alive?"

"Don't know. Mom said he left before the mattress cooled off."

Sonny rolled his eyes. "You're a bastard?"

He smiled. "I guess so. Some call me that and don't know it's true. Is that a problem?"

"A little. I'll need to get together with your mama and work out some kind of background for you. I see you left the 'applying for' space blank."

He smiled. "Didn't think you'd want to see son-in-law there."

"Don't get smart. For the time being, you're going to be Missy's driver. You'll start by driving her to Shreveport, but I'm putting down apprentice minister. That's what you'll be if everything checks out and we get your background cleaned up. Does that sound all right with you?"

"Very much so."

"Gwen."

She was behind Jamie Lee, but he could still picture her prime breasts as she answered in her sultry voice. "Yes, Sonny."

"Here's Mr. Vincent's application and W-9. Make a copy of the application for me. I want you to check out the references and employment."

Jamie Lee tried not to look at Gwen as she took the application from the reverend and mostly succeeded.

The reverend stood and held his hand out. "Thanks for coming by. You need to get going so you can get my baby to Shreveport on time. If I need anything else from you, I'll get in touch."

After shaking hands, Jamie Lee left, catching one last look at Gwen out of the corner of his eye.

* * * *

Reverend Riverton's driver, Walt, pulled up to 1242 West Nautilus Street in Tyler. It was an average looking home, maybe thirty years old. Considering there was no man of the house, the home appeared to be in good condition. He instructed Walt, "I don't want to raise any curiosity by parking the limo in front of the house, so find somewhere else to park until I call."

He stepped from the car, and as it pulled away, he walked up to the front door and pushed the doorbell. About thirty seconds later, Consuela Vincent opened the door and invited him in. For some reason, despite the fact that Jamie Lee was extremely handsome, the reverend expected Jamie Lee's mother to be unattractive and dumpy. She was neither. Ms Vincent was a petite five-three, shapely and striking.

As the reverend stepped in, Consuela smiled. "It really was you on the phone. I thought someone might be pulling my leg. Please follow me into the parlor."

"So, you know who I am?"

"Oh yes. I've watched your show from time to time. You have a very impressive presence."

When they entered the parlor, she invited him to sit, "Pleased be seated. I heated some water. Would you like some tea?"

He sat in what appeared to be an antique French provincial love seat. "That would be nice. Thank you."

She nodded, smiled and left, leaving Sonny to study well preserved antique furniture and wall hangings a few of which were of attractive gay nineties women in various states of attire.

After a short time, Consuela returned carrying a tray with a tea service and an assortment of herbal teas.

Sonny selected lemon, while Consuela picked chamomile, pouring hot water into both cups. Picking up her cup and saucer, she leaned back into the matching sofa and lifted her cup to her lips. "Now what can I do for you?"

"Jamie Lee has applied for a rather important job with our organization, therefore I need to ask you some questions. Would that be all right?"

She nodded, but said, "I'll let you know when it isn't. What would you like to know?"

He pulled a pocket recorder out of his coat pocket. "That's fine. I have a little recorder here. Would you mind if I recorded our conversation."

"No, that's all right."

The Televangelist I

Sonny decided to start with some softball questions. "How long have you and Jamie Lee lived in Tyler?"

"Twenty-three years. Jamie Lee was born here. Before that I lived in Dallas."

"What do you do for a living?"

"I'm an antique dealer."

"You have a store then?"

"Yes."

"In Tyler?"

"Yes."

"Tell me, does Jamie Lee have any siblings?"

"None living. My daughter, Lindsey, died at the age of four in 1975."

"I'm sorry. You say Jamie Lee was born here in Tyler? What hospital?"

Consuela straightened. "University of Texas Health Care Center."

"In what year?"

She took a sip of her tea. "1968. March 16th."

"I understand you don't know who Jamie Lee's father is. Is that right?"

She fidgeted and nodded.

"Most women know who fathered their children or at least have an idea. Could you please explain the circumstances under which Jamie Lee was conceived?"

Consuela's skin tone reddened and after squirming, she said in an imperious tone, "I hardly see how my son's father has anything to do with my son's ability to perform a job." She raised her gaze and met his. "Do you want to tell me what this is really about?"

The Televangelist I

"Yes. Do you have anything stronger than tea to drink?"

She smiled. Her smile was lovely. She was a lovely woman. "I have brandy." She rose, went to an armoire, and returned with a decanter almost full with amber liquid and two old fashioned glasses. She filled each glass half full then set one closer to him on the coffee table.

He picked the glass up and downed it in one gulp. Scrunching his mouth and nose, his pursed lips seemed to move in a circle on his face. Finally, he smiled at her. "That's good brandy."

"More?"

"Please."

She poured his glass three quarters full, and then picked up hers and drank half. "You were saying."

After downing half of his refill, he continued, "The job Jamie Lee is applying for is apprentice minister and husband to my youngest daughter."

Consuela's eyes rounded, raising brows halfway up her forehead. "My boy has been busy."

Sonny smiled. "Yes, he has." He snickered. "Maybe that's why I see a little of me in him. Can you see why I need to know everything? Believe me, I'm not out to embarrass you or anyone, but I cannot correct defects in his and your past if I don't know about them."

Consuela stared around the room, seemingly thinking. Then she looked at the reverend and spoke, "I see. So you and I would be related by marriage."

"Ah-huh. You could say that."

The corners of her lips curved into a demure smile. "Do you like antiques?"

He nodded. "Very much. Yes."

"Good." She poured his glass full, but left it sitting next to hers. Slowly, her gaze rose, locking with his. She smiled and patted the sofa next to her. "Would you like to sit next to me?"

He took a second to scrutinize her once more. With her long black hair and obsidian eyes, she was beautiful, and young looking for having a twenty year old son. She must have been a teen when Jamie Lee was born. He wasn't sure why she asked him to sit next to her, but he aimed to find out.

When he moved next to her, she laid her hand on his thigh. "I meant to ask, are you married?"

He wrapped an arm around her and rotated to a favorable position for a kiss. "Does it matter?"

She ran sexy, long nailed fingers down his cheek. "Not really."

Rising she held out her hand. "Since you like antiques, you really should see the ones I have in my bedroom."

"Walt?"

"Yes, Reverend Riverton."

"This is taking longer than I thought. Why don't you get a motel room and I'll call you at eight in the morning."

"Whatever you say, Reverend Riverton."

The Televangelist I

Chapter Six – Makeover

We need a translation that understands the needs of
America. A Biblical work that gets down and holy about
what to do about terrorism. Rev. Pat Robertson

A tall dark haired middle-aged man walked past
Gwen and into the Reverend's opulent, if ostentatious,
twenty-seventh floor corner office. "You wanna see me
boss?"

Sonny looked up. "Yes, hi Mike. I have a job for
you. Have a seat."

As Gwen brought his cup of black coffee he edged
the chair closer to the bosses desk and propped his feet
up on the corner of his desk. Sonny's jaw tensed like it
always did when he did that. Mike Hennings, his
million-dollar-a-year security director was the one
person who could get away with it, and he knew it.
"What you got boss?"

"Missy is engaged to a person of dubious
character with a Dalmatian background so spotty it's
almost solid black."

"Sounds surprisingly like Missy's father, before I
cleaned him up."

Sonny frowned. "Mike, you know I cleaned
myself up. You just tidied up some toxic problems in
my past."

Mike raised an eyebrow. "And you need me to disinfect his toxic background."

"Humph, more like radioactive. You'll earn your money on this one and it has to be quick. The engagement will be announced in October."

Sonny picked up a manila folder.

"What do you have there?"

"This is the only copy of my private file on young Jamie Lee Vincent." He passed the file to Mike, who lowered his topsiders to the floor and leaned forward, to receive it, then promptly leaned back in the chair and propped them up again as he perused the file. Obviously, discovering the photo, he quipped, "Handsome devil."

"Yes, smooth and personable, too. Mike, he has everything needed to be a big TV personality."

"Is that what you're doing, grooming him to take over for you?"

"Heaven's no, I'm not even sixty. I would like to turn the revival over to someone, though. That's a grind."

"Michael?"

Sonny shook his head. "He doesn't have the stamina. He couldn't finish the last tour."

"Too bad."

"I know. I actually need another minister to back-up Michael and me and I'm counting on Jamie Lee. You never know when the Lord will come for either one of us."

Mike continued to leaf through the file. "Sonny, save that crap for your flock."

The Televangelist I

Sonny sniggered. "Just practicing."

He shook his head. "Looks like your boy's a pussy hound, like somebody I know."

"Yeah, well—"

Mike's shook his head slowly as he read. "Contributing to the delinquency of a minor, three times; drunk and disorderly; malicious mischief; a bench warrant for ignoring two speeding tickets; assault. Your boy has a lot of problems and that doesn't even cover his juvenile record which is sealed."

Sonny gritted his teeth. "I know."

Mike's mouth dropped open and his eyes rounded in surprise. "Two rape complaints?"

Sonny leaned forward. "Date rape. I checked them out. The city prosecutor declined filing charges."

Mike sighed and shook his head. "Oh, oh! This is bad. Father unknown? How the hell—"

"I know. It wasn't easy, but I dragged the story out of the mother."

"Knowing you, the lady is good looking and the story came out over pillow talk."

"She is good looking. I won't comment on the rest."

Mike chuckled. "You don't have to. So tell me the story."

"The mother, whom I like, by the way—"

"I'll bet." Mike winked.

Sonny cast an intense stare. "You want hear this or not?"

He cast a playful grin. "I'm listening."

"Her name is Consuela. She and a boy named William Stewart ran away to San Francisco to join the hippies when he was eighteen and she was sixteen. From what she tells me Jamie Lee was conceived at the Monterey Folk Festival."

"Really, from Stewart?"

"No, he'd passed out from an exceptionally strong strain of hash." Sonny lifted a finger. "What I tell you can never be repeated. Understood?"

Mike frowned as if he'd been insulted. "Of course."

Sonny rolled his eyes and shook his head before he explained, "Our naive teen wouldn't take any drugs, so one of the nearby concert goers slipped LSD into her coke. Then as she started to get high and was grooving to the music, he told her the combination of sex and music would blow her mind. In what has to go down in the annals of teen-age stupidity, she laid him. In no time she was a beautiful naked sperm reservoir for any nearby stud that wasn't too high to get it up and they waited in line to fuck her."

Mike lowered his feet off the desk and leaned forward, apparently intrigued by his account of Consuela's ordeal. "How many?"

He shook his head again. "She can't be sure, but thinks maybe six. The girls that rescued her told her it was more like eight."

Mike's eyebrows rose. "Some girls rescued her?"

"Yes, three of them they'd been mesmerized by the incident, but didn't try to interfere until Consuela began to scream. They and their dates or boyfriends,

The Televangelist I

she wasn't sure, intervened, wrapped her in a blanket, and hustled her into a van. The boys went back to see if they could find anything—clothes, purse, shoes, anything—but they couldn't."

"What then?"

"She said they drove her to a commune. She started crying immediately wanting to go home, so the leader hit the men up for money and the girls for clothes. With seventeen dollars and sixty cents she boarded a bus in Fresno for Dallas."

Mike rubbed his hands together then clapped. "And nine months later Jamie Lee pops out." He laughed.

Sonny pointed at Mike and laughed too. "Bingo. Except it was eight months. Jamie Lee was a preemie."

"These people in the commune didn't stay in contact with her, did they?"

He shook his head, ardently. "Nope. She was a scared teenager they rescued and sent home."

"What happened to Stewart?"

"Consuela never saw him again. She blames him for what happened to her. Unbeknownst to her, he'd been drafted and missed his report date. He was caught shortly after that and turned over to the Army. He didn't come back from Viet Nam."

"Perfect. There's our father."

* * * *

As bad as his friend Jamie Lee had been, Tommy Parkson was the opposite. He was kind, generous, thoughtful and caring. Cheryl and Tommy had been going steady from the day of the revival some three weeks previous. She'd become convinced he loved her and she knew she loved him. That night he picked her up for their eighth date. He'd planned to take her to see a movie, but she had other plans.

Pulling the door of her parents' house closed and locking it, she dashed across the street and hopped into Tommy's older Camaro. "Guess what?"

Tommy gazed at Cheryl with his usual adoration. Then he chuckled. "No, telling wit you, girl. You're just full of surprises."

She leaned over the console, wrapped an arm around him and spoke under her breath, "My sister and her family went up to Oklahoma to visit her husband's parents."

"That's nice."

She kissed his cheek. "It is, and I'll tell you why."

When he didn't respond, she pursed her lips and continued. "I have to feed and take care of their dog while they're gone, so yours truly has the keys to their house."

"Yeah."

She pulled a package out of her purse and showed it to him. "You know what these are?"

She giggled when his eyes grew rounder and lit up. "Lifestyles? These are condoms."

She laughed. "Ah-huh, does that give you any ideas?"

"All kinds of ideas, but are ya sure?"

Nuzzling her lips into the crook of his neck, she kissed him and felt him shiver. "I've never been surer of anything in my life."

Tommy started the car and shifted into drive. "Den let's go. Gimme directions."

"Just head south, I'll guide you."

* * * *

Cheryl directed Tommy to the far south side of Tyler to a medium sized ranch style home on an acre west of U. Texas at Tyler. He parked in the driveway and they both got out of the car. Cheryl rushed up to him excitedly, and grasped his hand. "C'mon, let's go." She dragged him into the house, and after locking the door, led him straight to the master bedroom.

He was taken aback when she immediately started to undress. As she unbuttoned and shrugged her blouse off, Tommy broke his silence. "What are ya doing?"

She frowned. "What do you think? I'm getting undressed. I'm here to do one thing and by God I'm gonna do it. No teasing, no flirting." She continued undressing. Unfastening her bra, Tommy's heart jumped into his throat when she removed her bra and threw it atop of her blouse on a nearby chair. "Tomme-e-e. Get undressed. We're going to get naked, get in that bed and…make love."

Gawking at his love, he unbuttoned his shirt. By then, she'd pushed her jeans to the floor and stepped out of them. She looked like the best looking centerfold he ever saw in *Playboy*. "You're even more beautiful dan I imagined."

She smiled affectionately, as she removed her panties — her last item of clothing. "And you are slower than a snail in a hail storm."

The Televangelist I

His mouth dropped open as she strode toward him and placed her knuckles on her hips. "Don't you want to make love?"

With his shirt unbuttoned, he pulled one arm out of the sleeve and she pulled the shirt off his other arm. "Uh-huh, but I'm nervous."

She grasped his belt buckle. "I'm nervous too, but I want you more than anything. Don't you want me?"

He brushed her hand away. "Oh, yes, I want ya, but...

"What?"

He unbuckled his belt and dragged the zipper down. "I don't know what to do. I nevah done this before."

She looked up at him as she dragged his jeans down his legs. "Never?"

He shook his head as he stepped out of them. "Nope. I love you and I don't want to disappoint ya."

She rose and embraced him. "Don't worry, I love you, and this is my first time, too."

This surprised and pleased him. "You do? It is?"

She nodded. "Ah-huh."

Abruptly, he had trouble catching his breath as he realized her beautiful naked breasts pushed into his uncovered chest. Despite the anxiety he felt, his libido started to assert itself. After all, the girl of his dreams, who wanted him to fuck her, stood naked with her arms around him.

His half-hard manhood stirred when her long graceful fingers reached around his neck and pulled his mouth toward her upturned lips. As their lips

The Televangelist I

touched, a charge of erotic voltage zipped to his stiffening penis. When he nibbled on her warm, pliant lips, she moaned. Then as her tongue parted his lips and brushed across his teeth and he bloomed into full erection, she pulled away and squeezed him. "See, there's nothing to worry about."

His gaze devoured her. Focusing on her upturned medium sized breasts, his hands skimmed along her ribs, grabbed them and squeezed them. They were warm and, soft, but springy and her pink nipples, though standing upright like soldiers were pliable yet firm. They felt wonderful.

Gasping and sighing, she wrapped an arm around him as she stroked him with the other hand. "Come, let's learn about each other."

He nodded and they reclined on the bed.

* * * *

For the first time in her life, Cheryl woke up with a man in her bed. She turned on her side and stared at him. His sandy brown hair was disheveled and his eyelids covered his beautiful Columbia blue eyes, but his perennial smile was on his lips even as he slept. *Maybe he's dreaming of last night.* A smile crossed her lips as she recalled last night herself. This was the man who took her virginity — the man she loved.

As she expected, it hurt initially, but once he breached her virginal membrane, if started to feel good — real good. She even had an orgasm. She couldn't wait for tonight and more orgasms.

She leaned into him and tenderly kissed his lips, then slid out of bed. She smiled as she watched him

The Televangelist I

twitch and rub his hand over the spot she'd kissed. *God I love him.* She wondered as she went into the closet and borrowed a robe from her sister if they would marry. She hoped so. Slipping on a pair of her sister's slippers, she went into the kitchen to feed Carlos, the little Mexican Chihuahua. Afterwards, as her sister had instructed, she brought in the newspaper.

She hadn't developed a taste for coffee, so she poured a glass of orange juice from the refrigerator and sat down to read the Tyler Morning Telegraph. The paper wasn't very thick so it only took a few minutes to get to the religion section, where the heading made her jaw drop.

'Texas Cutie Breaks Engagement.'

'The religious sector underwent a bit of a shock when their sweetheart, bubbly, vivacious Missy Riverton broke her engagement with Reverend Donald Robson, son of Pat Robson, reputed to be the most watched televangelist in the world. Although it was announced as a mutual decision, there have been rumblings of a new beau for the last couple of weeks (lucky guy). It looks like we'll have to wait and see what develops.'

He pulled it off. The weasel weaseled his way into their family. Cheryl glanced at the accompanying photo. *What a beauty!* She read the caption.

The Televangelist I

'Former Texas Junior Miss, Missy Riverton, once Texas's most eligible bachelorette, is eligible again. Or is she?'

"What're ya doing beautiful?"

A chill ran through her. She jumped and her heart palpitated. Placing her hands on her chest, she took deep breaths to alleviate the sudden fright.

He wrapped an arm around her and kissed her cheek. "Sorry I didn't mean ta startle ya."

"It wasn't your fault. It's just that I became so engrossed in an article, I didn't hear you coming."

"What article's dat?"

Her forefinger pointed it out.

"Texas Cutie Breaks Engagement. Dat's Missy. You don't suppose…"

"That's exactly what I suppose. Your buddy's the mysterious Mr. X. Have you heard from him lately?"

His forehead wrinkled, his eyes looking upward. "Come to think of it, no. Not since he told me he was about to go into the Kilgore revival."

"And that was two weeks ago. Call him."

He frowned. "I thought ya didn't want me to associate with him?"

"I don't. Just find out what he's doing."

"All right, I'll be back in a minute."

Cheryl decided to make breakfast while he talked with Jamie Lee. She looked through the unfamiliar refrigerator and found bacon and eggs.

Pulling out a couple pans, she rustled them up in no time. Tommy hadn't returned, so she turned the

The Televangelist I

burners on simmer and went to see what kept him. Walking in she heard the end of Tommy's conversation with Jamie Lee.

"Well, I'm really happy things are goin' so well for ya."

"Thank you."

"I'll try."

"So long, Buddy."

* * * *

Jamie Lee terminated the call and threw the phone as hard as he could against the stone veneer fireplace in Missy's bedroom. The phone shattered into a dozen pieces. "Fuck." Tommy fucked Cheryl. *The son of a bitch had his cock in my woman.*

Missy called from the master bath. "What's the matter baby?"

"Oh, nothing, sweetheart. My phone stopped working and it pissed me off, so I smashed it against the wall."

She waltzed in dressed to the nines for a photo shoot. "Oh, poor baby. You might have to take an anger management class. I have to go now. How do I look?"

What's the matter with me? Why can't I be happy with Missy? Cheryl is hot, but she's no Missy. Missy is stunning — a ten! "Like the face that launched a thousand ships. Helen of Troy was a dog next to you."

She caressed his cheek. "You're sweet. Give me a kiss."

The Televangelist I

He purposely ignored her request, instead contorting his face into a mass of fake emotions. "I don't suppose you have enough time to suck my cock."

She looked at her watch and rolled her eyes. "I suppose. Just don't mess up my make-up or my hair."

"I won't. If my cock doesn't behave himself, I'll whack him."

She laughed as she knelt between his legs. "You better not whack him. That's my job."

* * * *

"Yeah, ever since the tent revival tour ended, he's been shacked up with her in her zillion dollar Dallas mansion while they decide what ta do with him. The engagement will be announced in two months en the wedding will be next March."

She grabbed his hand. "Let's go in the kitchen. I made breakfast and it'll get cold."

Seated at the table, Cheryl took a bite of bacon. "They'll announce the wedding will be in March. Go on."

Tommy, who'd donned his underpants and jeans, swallowed the forkful of scrambled eggs he'd put in his mouth and laid a hand over hers. "There isn't much more to tell ya, but I have somethin' else I'd like to say. Yesterday was the best day of my life."

She smiled. "Because we made love?"

"That's part of it, but somethin' else."

"That you lost your virginity?"

He laughed. "I did, didn't I? So did you. I almost stopped when ya started bleeding."

The Televangelist I

Cheryl snickered. "I would have brained you if you did. All right, tell me, why was yesterday the best day of your life?"

His grin was endearing. "Yesterday was da first time you said ya loved me and dat makes it easier to ask a question I've been meaning to ask you."

What a sweet man. They make love for the first time and what does he think is most important? That she told him she loves him. She lovingly caressed his cheek. "What's that?"

He lifted her hand and leaned down to kiss it. Then to her shock, he knelt. "Cheryl Alpern, love of my life, will you be my wife?"

She was too stunned to answer.

Thinking the worst, he said, "I understand if ya don't, since I don't have a permanent job, but I'm working at it. I have an interview with a Dallas TV station next week en I have an open job offer from a Louisiana Televangelist in Baton Rouge."

She felt the bubbling of emotion in her chest, first. Then the pain in her sinuses before the tears flooded forth. She rose, pulled him up and squeaked, "Yes."

"What?"

Her arms pulled him tight as tears deluged his shoulder with water. "I said yes! Yes, I'll marry you!"

He leaned back. "Really?"

"Really. I love you. How does Cheryl Parkson sound?"

"Pretty damned good. Correction, I just decided today is da *best* day of my life."

The Televangelist I

Cheryl laughed. Suddenly, she had the urge to be engulfed by Tommy's large hands. "Well, it's not exactly my worst day. Hurry up and finish eating. I feel like celebrating — in the bedroom.

He pushed his plate away. "I'm not hungry for food anyway."

She frowned. "No?"

"No really. I want ta try eating something else."

Cheryl raised an eyebrow. "Like what?"

"You!"

* * * *

"God dammit. Why'd you cum in my mouth? I asked you not to mess up hair or my make-up and who the *fuck* is Cheryl?"

Jamie Lee was mystified. "What are you talking about?"

She rose and stared at him. "When you came, you said Cheryl twice."

He shrugged. "She was a girl I went with for awhile."

She placed her hands on her hips. "Well, you must not like her much."

"Why?"

"You really don't remember what you said?"

He shook his head.

"I gotta go. I'll fix my hair and make-up at the studio." She picked up her purse and walked out, without a kiss or goodbye.

Jesus fucking Christ, what did I say?

* * * *

The Televangelist I

Jamie Lee was concerned. Not only had Missy avoided him by spending most of her time in her office, she hadn't said a word to him, made dinner or lunch for him. On top of that, she'd resisted his amorous advances.

Playing a video game, his mind churned as he did a slow burn. *Fuck this! Who the fuck does she think she is?* "Arrgh!" Suddenly, he rose and smashed the controls with his two hands. Heading toward her office with a tight-jawed grimace on his face, he planned to show her who was boss.

As he walked though the doorway, she looked up. *Don't screw up what you've accomplished so far. Remember, you draw more bees with honey than vinegar.*

Dwarfed by her oversized rosewood desk, her eyes were narrow and fiery, her nostrils flared. She looked extraordinarily beautiful. "What do you want?"

"I want you to come to bed with me."

"So you can shout out some girl's name. I don't think so."

"Babe, it was an accident. What did I say, anyway?"

Her eyes thinned even more as she snarled, "You said, 'so tell me, Cheryl, who's the cock sucker, now. I'm going cum right down your throat' and you did, only I'm not Cheryl."

Jamie Lee was stunned by the slip he'd made. "I thought I called her name twice?"

"You did. A little earlier you said, 'Cheryl, you're such a cunt.'"

The Televangelist I

He circled around her chair and started kneading her shoulders with his strong fingers. "Well, she was a cunt, but you're not. You're my sweet baby. I promise I'll never say anyone's name again, in the throes of passion, but yours and it'll be said in the name of love."

Her head went backward and she sighed. He sensed her muscles relax as a whimper of pleasure echoed from her throat. "Mmm, that feels good." Her head lolled around so he concentrated on her neck. "Mmm, that feels good, too! How can you be such an ass sometimes and so sweet the next?"

Though she couldn't see it, he shrugged. "I don't know, maybe I'm two people in one."

"Well, I like this one."

He stooped beside her and turned her executive chair to the left until she faced him. With her leg on each side of him, he ran his large hands up the inside of her thighs, under her skirt and rubbed her sensitive bud with his thumb through her silk panties. She closed her eyes and moaned.

"You know what I'd like to do?"

"I can guess. What?"

"I'd like to shave your pussy clean, and then spend the afternoon licking it."

She stood, helped him up, and embraced him. "All afternoon?"

He nodded. "Unless my tongue gets tired."

For the first time, she smiled. Then she took his hand and led him toward the door. "I'd like that too."

The Televangelist I

Chapter Seven – Cheryl and Tommy Marry

Keep a good attitude and do the right thing even when it's hard. When you do that you are passing the test.
Rev. Joel Osteen

Tommy was so excited he headed straight to Cheryl's parents' house.

Parking in the driveway, he flung the driver's door open and without even shutting it, rushed to the front door. When his fiancé opened the door he pulled her into his arms shouting, "I got it. I got it." Then his mouth crushed against hers in a passionate kiss.

When he pulled away, she asked, "Got what?"

With his arms around her waist, he leaned back to let his eyes focus. "The job as a camera man at KXAS TV Dallas. I start next Tuesday."

Cheryl's eyes grew to the size and shape of silver dollars and her mouth formed a perfect oh. "Oh, Tommy that's exciting, but…"

His eyebrows furrowed. "But what?"

Her cheek rested on his chest. "That means, you'll be moving away."

He shook his head. "It's only a hundred miles and I want ya to move there wit me."

Her nose and mouth scrunched. "But Tommy, My classes start at the community college in two weeks."

Tommy wrapped his large hands around her arms at the elbows. "See if ya can get your money back. You could enroll in college there."

Cheryl whined, "But Tommy, we're not married."

"I thought 'bout that. I don't have to be there for a week. If we took turns driving, we could get to Las Vegas in one day, get married, honeymoon there for three or four days en drive back in time for me ta get to work. What'dya think?"

She looked off as if she was thinking. "I don't know. It's all so sudden."

"All ya have to know is dat we love each other and we need to be together."

* * * *

She opened her mouth and looked upward. She'd never thought about running away to get married, but it would be so much easier. And they could be together right away. She gazed straight into his eyes and smiled warmly. "Okay, but let's take my car. It's newer and gets better gas mileage."

"Good idea, pack a bag. Den ya can follow me to my place before we go."

Surprise etched her face as her eyebrows rose into her forehead. "You want to go now?"

"May as well. The sooner we get there the longer our honeymoon would be."

She thought about it. She'd never done anything so...spontaneous, but it sounded like fun and they'd be together immediately. "All right, let's do it. You get going and I'll pick you up in." She glanced at her watch. "In twenty minutes."

As Tommy drove off, she rushed into the kitchen, and scribbled a note on the scratch pad next to the telephone. Then she raced into her bedroom and tossed as many clothes and toiletries in one suitcase as would fit. Before she shut the lid, she dropped her life savings — nineteen hundred dollars — in it."

She felt an adrenalin rush as she thought about what they were doing, hurried to her car and took off.

She smiled. When she returned she would be Mrs. Thomas Parkson.

* * * *

When Jamie Lee ambled into the Soldiers of the Lord offices from the elevator bank, Gwen looked up and smiled. "Hi, handsome."

He puckered his lips and hitched a kiss in her direction. "Hi, sexy."

Her smile brightened. "Go on in. He's expecting you."

As Jamie Lee entered the reverend's office, he rose and offered his hand. "Thanks for stopping by. Have a seat."

"Thank you, sir."

The reverend smiled. "I think since you're going to be my son-in-law we can dispense with formalities. Please call me Sonny."

"Thank you. I'll remember that." Jamie Lee sat and looked around.

"Would you like something to drink, coffee, orange juice, water?"

He lifted his left leg and crossed it over his right knee. "Orange juice would be nice, thank you."

The reverend picked the phone and punched in his secretary's number. "Gwen, would you bring Mr. Vincent an orange juice and get me a refill. Also hold my calls."

He said, "Thank you," hung up and turned his attention to Jamie Lee. While he'd been talking to Gwen, he noticed Jamie Lee looking around. "You've never been here before, have you?"

"No, sir I haven't. Quite a view. Mighty impressive."

"Thank you. A lot of hard work took place before getting to this point and if you live up to my expectations, you'll get an office like this, next to Michael's. Now, the reason I asked you here is — "

He paused as Gwen came in and handed the fresh cup of coffee to the reverend. "Here's your coffee sir."

"Thanks Gwen."

Turning toward Jamie Lee, she flashed a seductive smile and handed the glass of orange juice to him. "Here's your fresh *squeezed* orange juice, Mr. Vincent."

Taking the glass, he felt a jolt of desire as his fingers accidently rubbed against hers. "Thank you Gwen."

She puffed her sizable chest out. "You're welcome Mr. Vincent. Just let me know if you want anything else." He watched out of the corner of his eye as she sashayed out of the king-sized office.

The Televangelist I

When she'd left, Sonny resumed. "The reason I asked you here is we have reconstructed your background to an acceptable level."

Jamie Lee frowned. "Acceptable level? What does that mean?"

"It means, while you're no saint, we've changed your police record until the worst thing against you is the bench warrant for two unpaid traffic tickets and we found you a father.

"Yeah, who?"

"William Stewart."

Jamie Lee's brow furrowed and he pursed his lips. "My second cousin? Isn't that incest?"

* * * *

She smiled broadly, as she opened the door. "Why Sonny, what a pleasant surprise." She stepped back away from the opening. She batted her lashes and said, "Come in please."

He stepped in and walked to the couch they'd shared three days previous.

She straightened up the pillows and picked up the open newspaper on the coffee table. "Would you like some tea?" She asked as he sat down.

He glanced up at her. She was dressed neat and prim, in a peach blouse, ivory slacks, and open toed three-inch sandals, however, instead of her raven colored hair being down, this time she wore it up. "I don't suppose you have coffee?"

She cocked her head inquisitively. "Would instant be all right?"

He nodded. "That would be fine."

As she spun and headed toward the kitchen, he felt a stirring in his loins from her divinely shaped posterior and wondered if she would be amenable to a reprise of their liaison of a week ago.

A minute later, she returned with two cups of coffee and sat next to him.

As she handed one cup to Sonny, she inquired, "So, is your limo driver around?"

He took a sip of coffee, then answered her, "No, I drove myself this time. I hope my Lexus won't draw any undue attention."

"It shouldn't. I wasn't expecting to see you again. What brings you here?"

Sitting on the edge of the couch, he angled toward her so he could better see and talk with her. "Two things, first, why didn't you tell me the boy you ran off to California with was your cousin?"

She narrowed her eyes. "Does it matter?"

He smiled. "Normally I couldn't care less about your relatives, but this one we were going to try to make Jamie Lee's father."

Her lips formed a tight-lipped grin. "Hmm, sorry."

"Don't worry, we'll figure something out."

Her brows rose. "What's the second thing you came for?"

He laid his palm on the upper third of her thigh and squeezed. "Honestly, you. I can't get you out of my mind."

She smiled and rubbed a finger along his lips. "I did have a lot of fun with you." She grasped the hand on her thigh and rose. Tugging his hand in an upward direction, she snickered. "This time, I get to be on top."

* * * *

Sonny sighed. "Connie, you are amazing. If your son is half as sexual as you are, I can see why my daughter is so consumed with him."

She laughed. "Jamie Lee would be very angry if he knew I've been to bed with you."

"Really, you're a grown woman."

"I know, but he's very possessive — irrational. Tell me, do you really need to find a father for Jamie Lee?"

"I'm afraid I do. We have to make his background normal. A few blemishes are fine, even good since the public doesn't seem to like perfection, but being born out of wedlock, especially not knowing who the father is, is more than a blemish."

"Well, I have an idea."

An eyebrow dipped. "Go on."

"I don't know if this would work, but the leader of the commune they took me to, raped me before he sent me home. Jamie Lee would still be born out of wedlock, but at least he'd have a father and a good explanation."

Sonny's eyes narrowed. "I like that. It paints poor little Jamie Lee as a victim of a crime. Being the son of a rape victim sounds ten times better than a fatherless bastard. What's more, the right to life crowd would laude you for not terminating the pregnancy. What's this man's name and where was the commune?"

The Televangelist I

"The commune set just outside of Fresno. I think they called it Loving Ranch and I didn't know his name, but everybody called him Rance."

* * * *

Once Tommy and Cheryl obtained the necessary marriage license from the Clark County Clerk, they tied the knot in one of the ubiquitous Las Vegas wedding chapels. After spending the afternoon in their Circus Circus honeymoon suite doing what honeymooners do, they were famished, and visited the restaurant, planning to use one of the coupons from their honeymoon package.

While glancing through the menu, Cheryl began to look through her purse. "Damn it, I left the coupon on the night stand."

She started to get up, but Tommy stayed her with a hand. "Don't trouble yourself sweetheart. I'll get it. Go ahead and order. I'll have the French dip."

A couple minutes later, when the waitress arrived, she ordered. When the food arrived several minutes later, her brand new husband hadn't yet returned. When he'd been gone twenty minutes, Cheryl picturing him mugged and hurt in a hallway she became worried so she went to the hostess desk. "Hi, I need to find my husband. Is it all right if I leave my purse here while I look for him so you know I'll be back?"

The bright-eyed middle-aged lady smiled. "You go ahead honey, I trust you. And make sure you check those tables."

Cheryl looked around confused.

The Televangelist I

The lady chuckled. "In the casino—the twenty-one tables. Ninety-nine percent of the time that's where they are."

"Thanks, but this is our first time here. My husband doesn't gamble."

The lady patted her on the hand. "Whatever you say, honey. You go find that man of yours."

Shaken, she rushed up to their room. The coupon sat untouched on the nightstand. She grabbed it and, panicked, she rushed to the elevator bank. After what seemed like an eternity, she rushed from the elevator lobby into the casino. One by one, she scrutinized the hundred or so blackjack tables. Suddenly, she saw him walking like a zombie in the aisle that led to the restaurant. She ran after him. "Tommy. Tommy, I'm here."

When he turned, his appearance scared her. His skin appeared blanched, his eyes seemed glazed over, and he refused to meet her gaze. As she dashed up to him, tears fell from his eyes. "I lost it all. Everything I brought. Everything I have. Two thousand dollars. Our rent money, our honeymoon money. You married a fool."

For a split second she agreed, then banished the thought. This was the man she wanted, the man she loved. She took his hand, rose onto her tip toes, and kissed his cheek. "C'mon, our dinner is waiting."

"I'm not hungry."

"Well at least let me give them the coupon and leave a tip."

The Televangelist I

He nodded and they went back into the restaurant.

"Have a seat. Let me eat just a little of my BLT sandwich."

"How can ya eat? I just blew our honeymoon."

"I brought some money."

His eyes widened. "You did? How much?"

She glanced around and spoke under her breath. "Nineteen hundred."

His mouth fell open. "Let me have it. I need to win our money back."

"Absolutely not. You'd only lose it, too."

That night, Cheryl woke from a noise in the bathroom. She opened her eyes, but, except for sliver of light that escaped from under the bath door, it was dark. It was too dark to see if Tommy was in bed, but she knew he wasn't. She slipped out of bed and eased over to the bathroom. She opened the door slowly and saw the contents of her purse dumped onto the vanity top. In the mirror she could see him rifling through her suitcase, which he'd set on the toilet.

"What're you doing?"

Tommy had the look of a cheating husband caught in the act and in a way, he was. "I umm needed to borrow a couple hundred to win our money back."

Growing angrier by minute she rushed in. "I thought you were smarter than that." Pushing him away from her things, she zipped up her suitcase and turned to him. "What would you have done if you'd lost my money? Sold my car? And then what? I'm too

The Televangelist I

young to be a cocktail waitress. Maybe, I could be a topless dancer. Hell, why not a hooker?" She started to put her things back in her purse.

"What're ya doing?"

"I'm leaving. You can come or stay, but I'm leaving this home wrecker of a place."

"But...

She turned and snarled, "No buts. If you would have pulled this shit before I said 'I do,' I doubt I would have married you."

Suddenly, his demeanor changed as if he had an epiphany. His eyes cleared and he straightened. "Forgive me. Right now, I hate myself. Please don't hate me, too."

She studied him. He was tall and handsome. Yes, she still loved him, but she had no illusions. Though he possessed numerous positive qualities, he was also immature and weak. Maybe strength and maturity would come. She hoped so. But for now, and forever if he didn't change, she was going to be the head of this family.

The Televangelist I

Chapter Eight – Jamie Lee's Start
I have nothing to hide. I am a servant of the living God.
He is the only one I answer to. Rev. Benny Hinn

Trying not to stare too much at her cleavage, Jamie Lee winked and said hi to the sexy receptionist, "Hello doll face, the Boss wants to see me, again."

Thrusting out her chest, she rose. "Well, if it isn't Mr. Hottie." She ran her tongue across her upper lip. "I'll ring him."

Jamie Lee smiled, studying her as she made her call. She wore a terra cotta colored blouse with the top two buttons unbuttoned, revealing a lacy black bra beneath and a short, tight, black skirt.

"Reverend Riverton, Mr. Vincent is here to see you."

"Yes sir, I'll tell him."

Hanging up, she smiled seductively and raised an eyebrow. "Well, today's my lucky day. He wants me to take you down to the studio and show you around."

Jamie Lee smiled and waggled his eyebrows. "Must be my lucky day, too."

Nodding, she turned around and stooped on her black four inched, spiked heels to pick up her purse. She smiled coyly at Jamie Lee when she rose. "Are you ready?"

She wrapped her long nailed fingers around his forearm, when he held out his arm.

In the elevator lobby, she asked. "I need to visit the ladies room for a minute. Will you be all right?"

"Sure, take your time."

He watched her sashay and vanish into the ladies room. *The rev's got great taste. Too bad I'm engaged.*

He sensed his phone vibrating and pulled it from his slacks. "Hello?"

"Hey, buddy. It's Tommy. I just got back from Vegas and guess what."

* * * *

Gwen stood at the vanity, touching up her lipstick when she saw Jamie Lee enter in the mirror. She turned around, her hands and derriere resting against the vanity. She joked. "What's the matter, did I take too long?"

But he didn't laugh.

Instead, his eyes devoured her as if she was a steak and he hadn't eaten in a week. He reached out, placing his hands on her breasts. She gasped, but pushed into his hands. He eased right up to her. Sliding his hands down from her breasts and behind her, he groped her fine round ass and pulled her into him — into his hardness as he pushed into her softness. As his lips kissed her neck just below her ear, he whispered. "This *is* your lucky day."

She was going to ask coyly what he meant by that, when he crushed his lips to hers in a bruising kiss. As he slid his tongue past her teeth, she responded in kind, edging up onto the vanity and wrapping her legs

The Televangelist I

around him, while her fingernails raked his dark brown locks. When his lips parted from hers to work their way down her chest, she whispered in his ear. "I dreamed about this since I first saw you in Sonny's motor home."

* * * *

When Tommy and Cheryl got back, they found a reasonably priced one bedroom furnished apartment in south Dallas. They still had to go back to Tyler to get the rest of their belongings, but they spent that night in their new love nest.

Making love like newlyweds do until the wee hours of the morning, they didn't wake until ten-thirty. When Cheryl came out of the bathroom, she eased up to Tommy and put an arm around him. "Who were you talking to?"

"Jamie Lee. I told him about us."

Cheryl frowned. "I don't know if that was a good idea."

"Why? He'd find out sooner or later and then he be pissed because I didn't tell him."

Cheryl shook her head and sighed. "Yeah, I guess you're right. With Jamie Lee, you can never win."

* * * *

Gwen's red tipped fingers tunneled through his mane. "Oh baby, that was spectacular—even better than I dreamed."

"I know. It was fantastic. I'm sorry. Suddenly, I just had to have you. You won't get in trouble will you?"

"For what? I'm a single adult?"

The Televangelist I

Jamie Lee looked confused. "The reverend said you were taken."

"Yeah, I slept with him. It's how I got this job and these clothes, but we had no agreement. I never considered myself taken. She snickered. "But *you* could get in big trouble. You're engaged."

"I know. I shouldn't have, but something came over me and I had to fuck you."

Her head flew back and she chortled. "And I loved it. Don't worry. No one is the wiser and I'll never tell as long as you throw your cock my way every so often. By the way, who's Cheryl?"

He frowned. "Why do you ask?"

"Don't you remember?"

He shook his head. "That's why I'm asking."

"Hmm. Well, when you came you yelled 'cunt,' then you started to snivel, saying 'why'd you do it, Cheryl' over and over. I thought you were going to cry. Who is Cheryl, anyway?"

"Just someone I know."

* * * *

They got back to the executive office about an hour and a half after they left. Gwen called the boss. "We're back sir." She nodded to Jamie Lee. He pecked her on the lips and walked in.

"There you are. I was beginning to think you and Gwen went to lunch or something."

Jamie Lee was trying to think of an answer when the reverend continued. "What did you think of the studio?"

"Very impressive. First class."

The Televangelist I

"Thanks." The reverend, obviously pleased, leaned back and placed his hands behind his head. "Have you been studying the reruns of our shows, like I asked you?"

Jamie Lee sat down. "Yes sir, every day. I'm learning a lot."

"That's what I like to hear." He set three video tape cases on the desk close to Jamie Lee. Here're three more videos with four shows each."

Jamie Lee sat up and grabbed the cassettes. "Thanks, I'll take 'em home and watch them."

"Good. The reason I ask is now that we have your problem worked out, I want to bring you on board as a new cast member of Soldiers."

Jamie Lee's eyes narrowed with interest. "Really. He smiled. Who's my daddy now?"

"His name is Lawrence Miller. He was known as Rance when he impregnated your Mama."

Jamie Lee felt his jaw tense. "Is he still living?"

"Yes. He's an appliance salesman in Racine, Wisconsin."

"I'm glad that's settled. When are you going to have your next taping?"

"In three days. Friday at one, but for the next two days, I've retained a diction instructor to try to minimize your Texas drawl. Gwen will give you the details."

"Is that necessary?"

He nodded. "If you're going to be on TV speaking to people across the country, even the world, it is."

"You're the boss. When do you want me here on Friday?"

"Come in at ten-thirty so we can get you prepared."

"What do you mean?"

The reverend chuckled. "We have to fix your hair, get you made-up, and fit you for a suit."

"I'll be there."

* * * *

Two minutes after Jamie Lee left, the reverend's phone rang. "Hello."

"Sonny, this is Connie."

"Hi sweetheart. What can I do for you?"

"I received a mysterious, unsolicited offer through a Dallas real estate agent. In exchange for my business and house, which has a value, including inventory of no more than three quarters of a million, I'm to receive a six hundred thousand dollar, twelfth floor, high rise condominium and a successful Dallas antique store that does four million a year in business."

"Sounds like a good deal to me."

"It's too good of a deal. You're behind this aren't you?"

He smiled. "I can't comment on that, but I will tell you my penthouse is eight floors above the condominium and the view is magnificent."

He heard her laugh. "Are you trying to escalate our relationship?"

He chuckled. "I'm trying to avoid driving a hundred miles every time I want to fuck you."

The Televangelist I

She laughed. "Hmmm, the fringe benefits sound interesting."

"Are you going to accept it?"

"I'd be a fool not to, wouldn't I?"

* * * *

Jamie Lee came in the garage door and heard Missy working out in the exercise room. He walked up to her and kissed her cheek as she walked rapidly on the treadmill.

"Hi Babe, guess what?"

"No telling with you."

Jamie Lee stared at her.

When he didn't continue, she frowned and said, "What?"

He laughed. "God, you're hot. Even your sweat smells good."

She scrunched her face, but followed that with a giggle. "And you sir, are full of it and the polite word would have been perspiration."

"Even your perspiration smells good, but not as good as your pussy."

Her mouth dropped open as she rolled her eyes. "You're insufferable. Are you trying to get me horny?"

He shrugged. "You're my little nympho. You're always horny, aren't you?"

"Around you I am. So what's your big news?

"I'm going to be on the show with you tomorrow."

"That's fabulous." She turned off the tread mill and hugged him. "I love you." She snickered. At least this version of you. I'll tell you what. I'm going to jump

The Televangelist I

rope for two minutes, after which I'll need to take a shower. If you happen to be there when I get in, who knows what'll happen."

"I think I'll get the shower nice and toasty for you."

The Televangelist I

Chapter Nine – A Star is Born

*What we saw on Tuesday (9/11), as terrible as it is,
could be minuscule if, in fact, if in fact God continues to lift
the curtain and allow the enemies of America to give us
probably what we deserve.* Rev. Jerry Falwell

Jamie Lee was nervous as a cat in a dog kennel as he waited offstage for the reverend to get around to introducing him. When he and Missy had arrived, she and the director briefed him on what he was supposed to do, act and say. Next, he underwent one-hour hairstyle and make-up sessions, after which he changed into a wardrobe someone had provided for him.

He studied as much of the live audience as he could see from where he stood. They seemed friendly enough.

Of course they're friendly, they're the flock. A truer term couldn't have been written in the bible. They were like a gathering of sheep, believing everything they were told and one day he'd be doing the telling.

"Dear Christians, we have a brand new reborn sinner with us today. I'm proud to say my daughter, Missy, personally saved this young man, so I'm going to let her tell you about it."

The Televangelist I

He stepped to the side and the spotlight shifted to her. "Ooh, this is so exciting." She paused while the audience clapped. "First, I'll tell you about it and then I'll introduce him. I was with Michael, Bobbie Sue and her husband Grant on a tent revival in Tyler, Texas when I met Jamie Lee. From the minute I saw him, I knew he was a sinner. He was smug and arrogant, but he had a presence about him, a magnetism that couldn't be ignored and I thought, wouldn't it be wonderful if someone with his charisma could be brought to the side of God.

"He'd never been to a revival, so I invited him and he came. Well folks, he must have felt the spirit of the Lord, for when it came time to be saved, he stood up. Well I'll tell you, for everyday sinners, our tent revival baptism works fine, but our boy was a serious sinner and I suspected the Lord wanted me to give him the V.B.S. treatment." She winked and went on, "That's Very Big Sinner treatment," She was interrupted by laughter and clapping. When it calmed down she proceeded, "so I had him sit down until the revival was over and then with the help of Bill our muscle bound Sergeant at Arms, I filled a bathtub full of holy water and gave him the *full* Soldiers of the Lord treatment.

Again, she was interrupted by laughter and applause. "Well, I have to tell you folks, the concentrated spirit of God's loving grace was so strong, we both felt ecstasy."

Jamie Lee couldn't help but snicker on the ecstasy part.

The Televangelist I

"Anyway, Jamie Lee became so overwrought with emotion, he couldn't thank me enough, and he went on to say he wanted to dedicate his life to Christ. And so I present to you, God's newest convert. Folks, how about a nice round of applause to make Jamie Lee Vincent feel welcome."

Jamie Lee ran out on the stage waving and smiling as if he was already a star. The standing ovation was deafening, prolonged, and seemed to increase as he kissed Missy on the cheek. He grabbed a mic from the stand and said, "Thank you, thank you." The clapping diminished, but didn't stop. He shouted over it, "Thank you. I feel great! How about you?" More loud applause died a little when he gave the quiet down sign by holding his right hand out and lowering it. "Like Missy told you, my name is Jamie Lee Vincent, and ladies and gentlemen, *I have been saved!* It's a great feeling knowing you walk in God's grace and I owe it all to our little honey, Missy Riverton." Standing sustained applause followed his pronouncement.

When the audience quieted, he continued, "My hero," Jamie Lee hitched his head toward the reverend, who was still on stage to his left, "Reverend Sonny Riverton, has given me the opportunity to bear witness to all of you. To testify about God's acceptance and forgiveness. Folks, I was lost. I always got into trouble, couldn't find a decent job, I was obsessed with the pleasures of the flesh, and I even toked a little hash." Laughter filtered from the crowd. "Then again things could have been worse considering I started out life in the hole. Folks, if I stick around as I hope to, y'all will find out anyway, so I'm going to get it out in the open—I'm a bastard. Folks, I was born to a teenage mother out of wedlock, the product of rape."

It seemed as if there was one huge gasp and then someone hit the mute button on the audience. Jamie Lee worried that he'd blown it. After ten seconds of silence, one brave soul started clapping. Immediately, another joined in, followed by ten more, and soon everyone clapped, then everyone stood. Someone yelled, "Jamie Le-e-e, Jamie Le-e-e." Soon everyone joined in the chant. At that moment, he knew he owned the audience and he was amazed at how easy it was.

After five long minutes of wooing the flock, Jamie Lee bade goodbye and the reverend took center stage. "Well folks, how did you like Jamie Lee?" Again the throng rose, clapped and when he asked if they would like Jamie Lee to come back, the affirmation was seismic. A star had been born.

After the show ended, the reverend brought out the bubbly and a mini celebration ensued. "Son you knocked 'em dead today. I wouldn't be surprised if they ran me out of town in favor of you, after today."

Jamie Lee took the offered flute of Dom Perignon from his boss. "Never happen, sir. You're 'the man.'"

Sonny tossed his head back and chortled. Missy strolled up. "What are you laughing about daddy?" Both men slung an arm around her.

"Oh, I joked about how our congregation found a new hero today and won't want me around anymore."

The Televangelist I

"And I told him it would never happen. That he's irreplaceable, not to mention Michael would be the next in line."

Jamie Lee couldn't help, but notice how strangely Missy and Sonny looked at each other and how the reverend shook his head ever so slightly and mouthed, "No."

He turned to Jamie Lee. "I don't know son. We'll have to see if they'll let me stay after we announce your engagement in two months. What a powerful Christian team you two make."

Later, as everyone started to leave the improvised celebration, Sonny came up to Jamie Lee. "Son, I asked Missy to take you somewhere tomorrow. With you being a member of the show now and soon to be a family member, there are things you need to know."

* * * *

The next day was Saturday. With Jamie Lee in the passenger seat, Missy drove her BMW convertible, top up, through Dallas and south along Interstate 35E.

As Jamie Lee watched the central Texas countryside wiz by he asked Missy. "Where are we going, baby?"

She shifted her gaze to Jamie Lee for an instant. "To Waxahachie. Ever been there?"

He laughed. "Been there? I never even heard of it. Is it far?"

Just then, they passed a mile marker that read, 'Waxahachie, 15 miles.'

"Nah, we're almost there."

"What's there?"

The Televangelist I

"Oh, it's a pretty little town with some very nice Victorian architecture. You'll see."

"I meant why are we going there?"

"I know baby. It won't be long."

Twenty minutes later, Missy pulled into a small parking lot adjacent to a large Victorian residence, which appeared to be converted into some sort of nursing home. She parked in a space reserved for administration and got out. "Are you coming?"

Jamie Lee hopped out and looked the mediaeval looking edifice over. Missy came around the car, grabbed his hand, and tugged him toward the building as he studied the structure. Tyler too, had many Victorian style homes, but the complexity of this building with its huge wrap- around porch, multiple turrets, and fancy dormers was like nothing he'd seen before.

As they strode around to the front of the building, he read the sign, 'Loving Rest, Convalescence and Assisted Living Facility.' "Do we own this?" He inquired.

"Yes, the church owns lots of things, including my home, which you are currently living in."

As they walked in, the receptionist stood. "Miss Riverton. What a pleasant surprise."

Missy nodded. "Thank you. Is Molly in?"

"I believe so, would you like me to ring her?"

Missy raised a hand to stop her. "Don't bother we'll head back to her roost." They walked under a magnificent staircase and down a dark hallway to the office of Molly Madden, Facility Administrator.

Molly, an attractive, middle-aged African American, rose, but Missy put her at ease. "Hi Molly, don't fuss about us. I just wanted to let you know we were here, before we head back. It's all right isn't it?"

"Of course. And who might this be?"

Missy blushed slightly. "I'm sorry. This is my fiancé and love of my life, Jamie Lee Vincent. Jamie Lee this is Molly Madden, Loving Rest's administrator."

Still standing, they shook hands. "Pleased to meet you."

"Likewise, I'm sure."

Molly glanced back to Missy. "So the rumors are true?"

Missy smiled coyly. "Yes, for once. Well, we better get going. I'll visit with you more next time I'm here."

Missy took his hand and as they turned to leave Molly said, "It was nice to meet you."

Jamie Lee flashed Molly his charm smile. "It was my pleasure."

Missy seemed to know exactly where to go. They backtracked to the lobby and ascended the ornate staircase to the second floor. They walked past several numbered rooms to a nurse's station in what appeared to be a gutted out room. She walked up to the counter and addressed the nurse as she looked up. "Hi, I'm Missy Riverton."

The nurse answered, "Yes, Ms. Madden just called and said to expect you. You know where they are?"

"I do. Thank you. We won't be a bother."

The Televangelist I

From that point, Missy led him further down the hall, into room 214. A slightly built blonde woman, perhaps in her early fifties looked up. "Are you from the...of course not, you're much too young."

Missy let go of Jamie Lee's hand and stepped up to the woman. She grabbed a chair and sat next to her. "It's Missy, Mom. Don't you recognize me?"

The woman looked at her with renewed interest. "Missy? Oh, my. You've gotten so big. And lovely. It seems like only yesterday, you were a pretty little girl in pig tails." She gaped at Jamie Lee, her brows dipped. "Who's this? He's not one of them, is he?"

"No, Mom." Missy waved for him to come over.

When he stood beside them, she continued, "This is Jamie Lee, the man I'm going to marry." She glanced at him. "This is Bernice Riverton—my mother."

They visited Bernice, who regularly slipped in and out of cognition for another twenty minutes. When they left Jamie Lee asked, "What's wrong with her?"

"I'll tell you all about it, but we have one more to visit. I'm cold. Could you put your arm around me?"

As they walked back to room 205, he wrapped an arm around her. Indeed, her petite body shook. The person they saw next shocked Jamie Lee. It was Missy's brother, Michael, whom he hadn't seen since that first revival in Tyler, but in all the excitement since their engagement, he hadn't even missed. The minute she saw him tears formed in her eyes. Though he appeared to be sleeping, she rushed to him. Holding his hand, she kissed him again and again.

The Televangelist I

Michael was a shadow of the vibrant man he'd seen in Tyler. He was gaunt and sallow. There were sores on his arms and face. He was hooked up to an IV and an electronic monitoring device. They didn't stay long. Missy began weeping—a little at first, then uncontrollably. She was in agony so Jamie Lee helped her up. With an arm around her, he led her out, down the stairs and back to the car.

Jamie Lee took the car keys from her purse and drove home. He had question after question he wanted to ask, but she was in no condition to answer them. By the time he noticed her sniffling had ceased, she'd fallen asleep.

She was still sleeping when they got home. He pulled in the garage, carried her into the house and to their bedroom. After setting her on the bed and removing most of her clothes, she woke. She glanced around and realizing where they were, wrapped her arms tightly around him. "Please, Jamie Lee. I need you to make the ache go away. Please make love to me."

That night she lived up to his nympho comment when they made love until one a.m.—for four hours—and wanted more. Even though he said, "Tomorrow," as he rolled over, she wrapped an arm around him and spooned in behind him, before falling asleep.

Chapter Ten – Skeletons

My message is a message of hope that God is a good
God, and that no matter what we've done, where we've been,
God has a great plan for our lives. Rev. Joel Osteen

Jamie Lee woke before Missy. He got up, showered, shaved, slipped into a pair of warm-up pants, and went into the fancy kitchen. They'd missed dinner last night, so he was hungry. Not being much of a cook, he looked in the refrigerator for something he could put together with little effort. He settled on toast and jelly. As he took his first bite, the doorbell rang. He went to the front door, peeked through the peephole, and saw a young woman. Missy had mentioned a cleaning lady would come every week, so this had to be her.

He opened the door and looked her over. She was a pretty girl, maybe in her early twenties. "Maria?"

She looked him up and down, smiled and nodded. "Si,"

As she stepped through the door, he asked, "Do you speak English?"

"Si."

"Good. Miss Riverton is still asleep."

"No, I'm not." Missy walked into the kitchen in shorts, a scrimmage shirt and running shoes. "Hi Maria. This is my fiancé, Jamie Lee."

She turned to him and said in broken English, "Nice to meet you."

He smiled. "Same here, Maria."

Missy eased up to him and pecked him on the lips.

He wrapped an arm around her waist and kissed her back lightly on the lips. "I've been waiting for you to wake up. I have a lot of questions."

"I'll be in the work-out room. When you finish your toast, come in and I'll answer what I can."

Jamie Lee gobbled his toast down as he watched Missy's hot little ass shift back and forth as she sashayed into the family room. "Wait up, I'll be right with you," he exclaimed with his mouth still half full."

She partially turned and paused until he caught up, leaving Maria to do her thing while they headed to the exercise room.

Jamie Lee leaned against a wall as Missy mounted a stationary bicycle. "I want you to know I'm sorry I fell apart on you yesterday. It really upsets me to see Michael like that."

"It's all right. I understand." His lips curled into a naughty smile. "Plus it led to some of the best sex I've ever had."

She laughed. "I'm glad you enjoyed it, I probably would have enjoyed it more if I hadn't been so blue. What did you want to know?"

"Well for starters, I want to know what's wrong with him."

Missy bit her lip. "Michael has AIDs. Daddy has spared no effort trying to get him better and we thought we turned the corner and then this."

Jamie Lee felt sick. He didn't know much about the disease, but he knew that most everyone who got it seemed to die a miserable death. "How? He seemed so healthy in Tyler. What happened?"

Missy wiped a tear away. "He was in remission, but his partner was sick and dy—"

"Partner!" Jamie Lee screeched, "Michael is gay?"

She nodded. "I'm afraid so, and if there's one thing you don't want to be in a fundamentalist evangelical church it's gay. Especially, if you're son of the minister. Unfortunately, his partner died shortly after I saved you, and Michael fell apart. When we headed to Shreveport, he went to Dallas. Shortly, after he attended Ron's funeral he got sick again and in a week, he was back in Loving Rest Home. He's been there ten days now."

Jamie Lee was surprised. He actually felt a pang of sorrow for Michael and Missy. Usually, he only felt emotional about things that affected him. "That's shitty, really shitty."

Sniffling, Missy agreed, "It is." Then she broke down. Both hands wiped the flood of tears from her eyes as she stopped pedaling. When Jamie Lee sidled up to her, placing a reassuring hand on her waist, she flung her arms and most of her weight around him and wept on his shoulder. With one hand encircling her waist, he snaked his other hand under her thighs and lifted her off the bike. He surveyed the large well-

The Televangelist I

equipped room, and noticed the champagne colored, Naugahyde couch adjacent to the ballet bar and mirrored wall.

He set her there and tried to sit up, but her arms held him in place while her mouth sought his lips. When he returned her kiss, her hands roamed his back, working their way down to his taut buns. In return, his hands glided up her bare ribs, under the hem of her scrimmage shirt and kneaded her breast. Cresting her back, she pushed her breasts into his hands. Untying the drawstring of his athletic pants, she pushed them down, until his rigid maleness popped out like a jack-in-the-box.

He pulled away from their amorous kiss as she stroked him and gasped from the pleasure that coursed through him. Then with his eyes closed, he groaned as Elysian warmth and wetness encircled his erection.

When they'd finished on the couch, they went into the shower and made love again. Afterwards while they toweled off, Missy reminded him, "I have to hurry. I have to be at our church by eleven."

"What about me?"

"You can come, but not with me. Not until we're officially engaged in eight weeks."

"I wish we could go there like a couple, now."

A sympathetic expression formed on Missy's pretty face. She ran her knuckles lightly across his cheek. "I know sweetheart, but don't fret, time will go fast. Oh, I forgot to tell you. Daddy wants to see you in his office tomorrow."

The Televangelist I

"What time?"

He didn't say."

* * * *

"Cheryl." Tommy yelled.

"What?"

"Come here, you hafta see this. That cute blonde girl just introduced Jamie Lee on the Soldiers of the Lord show."

Cheryl came in and sat next to Tommy on the used couch they bought. "I'll be. It is him. I'll bet he'll be good at this too. It's right up his ally."

Tommy laid a hand across her bare thigh. "Quiet babe, I wanna hear."

They sat in silence for roughly five minutes, and then Tommy exclaimed, "Hot damn, he was really good, wasn't he?"

"Unfortunately, yes. It doesn't surprise me, but he's still a bastard."

"Baby, what you got against Jamie Lee anyway?"

She wrapped an arm around him and snuggled her head into the crook of his neck. "Tommy, you're a sweet man and that's why I love you, but you have to see Jamie Lee for what he is."

Tommy rose and twisted around to her. "What are you talking about?"

"Face it sweetheart, Jamie Lee is out for Jamie Lee and no one else."

"Oh, yeah I'll bet if he was in charge I could go to him and get a job as a cameraman."

"Well, he's not in charge, so we'll never know, will we?"

The Televangelist I

* * * *

Monday morning, Jamie Lee headed to the nearest Seven Eleven and picked up copies of *The Dallas Morning News* and *The Fort Worth Star Telegraph*. He wanted to see if either newspaper had written anything about his debut on 'Soldiers of the Lord.'

When he got home, Missy waited for him. "Daddy called. He wants to see you in his office before noon today."

He nodded. "I'll go right after I read these papers. I want to see if they say anything about yesterday's show."

"All right, I'll tell him you'll be there. Just make sure you make it before noon. He has a meeting to go to afterward."

It turned out both papers had front-page stories in the religious sections. The Dallas Moring News article made him smile. Under the headline 'A **Star is Born**,' followed a stellar three-hundred-word article praising him as a 'new prophet of God.'

Unfortunately, what the *Dallas Morning News* gaveth, *The Fort Worth Star Telegram* tooketh away. Above the byline of Danielle White, the headline glared, "**Soldiers' Recruit Bastard Preacher**.' The following article slammed the nascent televangelist, starting with, 'Soldiers of the Lord,' unveiled a new cast member Sunday — self-proclaimed bastard, Jamie Lee Vincent. Terms like arrogant, pompous, and preening, made Jamie Lee's blood boil, even though the article finished on a positive note. 'Although his brief sermon bored this writer, Jamie Lee displayed

The Televangelist I

flashes of charisma, even brilliance. That is why I'm reserving final judgment until he matures as a preacher and a person.'

Hmmm, Danielle White. I'll remember that name.

* * * *

"You wanted to see me boss?"

Sonny looked up and smiled. "Well, if it isn't the new star in the heavens, Jamie Lee Vincent. Have a seat. Can I get you anything?"

"I'll take a Coke if you have it."

"You got it." He picked up the phone and punched in Gwen's number. "Bring Jamie Lee a Coke, will you?"

"No, I'm fine, thank you. I have to leave for my meeting in a few minutes."

The reverend hung up, and leaned forward and set both elbows on the desk. "I have a last-second meeting to attend, so I have to leave in five minutes, but I just wanted to tell you a couple things in person. Even though we still had two taped shows ready to go ahead of the one we taped Friday, we ran it yesterday."

Jamie Lee was pleasantly surprised. "I know, I read the reviews this morning."

"The studio audience loved you and the reviews weren't bad, but I wanted to know what viewers thought, so I hired a marketing company to poll the viewers.'"

"You did? How did I do?"

Sonny rose and his endearing smile grew wider — absolutely gleeful. Just as Gwen walked in with Jamie Lee's Coke, he stuck his hand out and exclaimed, "You knocked their socks off, son." He paused while Jamie Lee shook his hand and took the Coke from Gwen, then continued as she left. "You did even better than I'd hoped. Eighty-six percent loved you, twelve percent were undecided and only two percent didn't care for you."

Jamie Lee felt a pang of anger at the two percent who didn't like him, but was pleased overall. "That's fantastic."

"It is. You know what that means, don't you?"

"We need more shows?"

The reverend smiled and pointed at him. "Right you are; so starting Friday afternoon, we're going to tape six new shows. On the seventh show, we'll announce your engagement to Missy so we'll tape it seven weeks from this Friday. Now, I don't suppose you can afford an engagement ring worthy of my baby. Can you?"

"Probably not."

"Well you need to get her a nice ring. SOL has an account at Renaissance Jewelers. He handed Jamie Lee a business card. Go by there and pick something nice for her—say around twenty-five grand and tell them I said to give you the wholesale price plus ten. Any questions?"

"No, that about covers it."

"Good, Missy tells me she took you to see Michael and Bernice on Saturday?

Jamie Lee nodded. "Tragic, sir. My heart and prayers go out to you."

The reverend stood and came around the desk. Jamie Lee stood too and the reverend patted him on the shoulder. "Thank you. I have to leave shortly. I want to assign Michael's office to you, temporarily. I pray to God, I get to take it back from you and have to build you an office of your own, but for now it's going to be yours. I was going to show it to you, however since I have to leave, Gwen can show you and give you the keys."

"Thank you, sir. Sir?

"Yes?"

"Missy told me about Michael, but she never told me about Bernice."

He rubbed his chin. "Hmmm. All you need to know for now is she had a nervous breakdown. I have to go." Touching him lightly in the back, he urged Jamie Lee toward the door.

"Gwen, I'm running late would you show Mr. Vincent his new office. Answer any questions he may have and make sure he has all the keys."

"Yes, Reverend Riverton."

When he left, Gwen reached for a set of keys and grabbed Jamie Lee's hand and led him toward Michael's former office. "Are you ready to see your new office and our sleeping quarters?"

"What are you talking about?"

"You'll see."

When they entered the office, the drapes had been closed, so it was dark and musky. Jamie Lee walked behind the desk and pulled the drapes open. The room lit up and instantly and he smiled. "Love that view."

"Hold out your hand, palm up." Gwen dropped a key in it. "That's the key to the office." Then she dropped a second key in it. "That's the key to your desk and personal file cabinet." She held a third key up. "This key is for the liquor cabinet."

"I want to show you something." She grasped his hand again and led him to a door on the wall that abutted the reverend's office, or at least that's what he thought.

"We're going into reverend's office?"

She smiled knowingly at him and shook her pretty head. She opened the door and with a wave of her hand invited him in. Jamie Lee stepped into a small, but lavishly appointed bedroom. "What is this?"

"I told you. Our sleeping quarters." Her gait had a spring as she stepped over to the bed. She knelt with one knee upon it, suggestively sticking her ass in the air. He stood directly behind her admiring the form of her buttocks. She tilted her head to the left and looked behind her, directly at Jamie Lee. Now that you're my boss, too, is there anything, anything at all you'd like me to do."

"I can think of a few things, but tell me, other than the obvious reason for this room, what is the stated reason?"

She rolled over and sat upon the bed, bouncing up and down a couple times. As she started to unbutton her teal and vermillion print blouse, she said, "There are two rooms. Reverend Riverton has an identical room and that's where I lost my 'Soldiers of the Lord' virginity." She slipped the top of her blouse over her shoulders and wriggled them until gravity took it to the bed.

Next, she undid the snap in the back of her lacy red bra. "The popular explanation for these fuck rooms is they are a place to take a nap should you get tired. Or, God forbid, should you work late and not feel up to driving home, you could spend the night."

With the bra hanging loosely in front of her breasts, she lifted one and displayed it to Jamie Lee. "That's right. You haven't seen these yet. Reverend Riverton says they're the absolute best he's ever seen."

Her breasts mesmerized Jamie Lee. They were perfect, with their light areolas and perky nipples." She slipped her arms through the straps of bra and let it fall into her lap. Displaying it with one hand, she flung it over her shoulder as she leaned forward and slipped a four inch, red, spiked heels off with the other.

Jamie Lee was tantalized when she leaned forward, and her beautiful breasts swung away from her chest, swaying to the motion of her hand removing her heels. "Jamie Lee, you have no idea how wet I am. I've been thinking about having your big dick in me — spreading me, stretching me and rubbing the walls of my pussy, since Reverend Riverton asked me to show you the office." She reclined onto her back and lifted a single well-turned leg straight into the air. "That's another thing Sonny likes, my legs. What do you think?" She raised the other leg and moved them alternately forword and backward.

"You're legs are wonderful. You're wonderful."

The Televangelist I

She spread her legs wide and smiled, then lifting her head to look at him, she frowned. "What're you waiting for? Aren't you going to get undressed? Believe me, I want to see you naked as much as you want to see me naked."

His fingers undid the first and second buttons of his shirt and moved to the third. "Sorry, I became captivated by your sexy strip tease."

She closed her legs and moved them forward allowing their weight to raise her into a sitting position. With his shirt removed, his hands moved to his slacks. "That's better." She stood and eased her short, solid, red skirt from side to side down over her hips, thighs and down, ultimately piling around her sexy feet. She stepped out from her skirt and kicked it to the side, leaving just her lacy red panties. "I'm almost naked, you'd better hurry up."

He kicked his shoes off so he could get his slacks off, and then stepped out from them.

Her hand grasped one of her breasts and lifted it while simultaneously lowering her lips and tongue to her hardened nipple, then sucking on it and circling it her tongue. "Reverend Riverton says he could suck on these for hours. Would you like to do this, while I take my panties off?"

He didn't even answer her. He sat beside her surrounding her nipple with his lips, while she reached into his shorts. "Oh, my."

Chapter Eleven – Vice
*There are two great forces, God's force of good and the
devil's force of evil, and I believe Satan is alive and he is
working, and he is working harder than ever.*
Rev. Billy Graham

Consuela looked out over West Dallas. She could
even see the high rises of Fort Worth beyond the Dallas
Fort Worth International Airport. "Oh, Sonny the view
is magnificent. I don't know how to thank you."

He snickered. "We'll think of something. I
thought you'd at least have a bed up here by now."

She turned to face him and smiled. "I can see
what's on your mind."

He threw his head back and laughed. "I'll admit
that's on my mind, but I was talking about having a
bed to sleep on. When does your furniture arrive?"

"Early tomorrow morning. I don't suppose I could
impose upon you to spend the night."

"Of course, I was just going to suggest that." He
eased into her. "I like your hair down." He rubbed his
nose across hers Eskimo style. And your perfume.
What is it?"

"Gorgio and it's cologne. I told you that before."

"I forgot." He nestled his nose near the top of her
neck and inhaled. "I love the fragrance." He kissed her

tenderly on the lips. "I like the aroma of something else on you, too."

"I know. You told me. By the way, I shaved for you."

"Really? Let's go up to my penthouse then. We can have dinner in bed and I have a video tape of our last show I'd like to show you."

"I'd like that."

* * * *

Jamie Lee woke in a stupor. *What's that noise?* He looked at his watch and sat up quickly. "Oh, my God, it's ten after eight." He reached for and checked his beeper. Two messages, both from Missy.

He heard Gwen giggling and turned his gaze to her, lying naked, next to him. He couldn't decide who looked better naked, her or Missy, they were both exquisite. "What are you laughing about?"

"You. You aren't even married yet and you're already pussy whipped."

"Yeah, well, if I pull this anymore, I might not even make it to the altar."

She laughed. "Just tell her you were celebrating, knocking the viewer's socks off by fucking Gwen's socks off. You did you know? You were magnificent. You are magnificent."

"Very funny." *How did I end up with two beautiful insatiable women? How am I gonna keep two nymphos happy?*

He jumped out of bed and dressed in two minutes. "Sorry to fuck and run. Damage control, you know." He leaned down and kissed her. "Thanks, it

The Televangelist I

was even better than I thought it would be and I expected it to be spectacular."

Jamie Lee hopped out of the elevator and raced to his car, a sixty-eight Pontiac GTO, gas-guzzler. Heading straight to Renaissance Jewelers, he picked out an engagement/wedding ring set, a fancy diamond bracelet and something small for Gwen.

If looks could kill, Jamie Lee would be gasping for breath from the stare Missy gave him when he got home.

"Hi, sorry, I didn't know you were going to cook dinner tonight."

"Well, I did. It's probably overcooked and dry by now. Where were you? I called twice and left messages."

"I'm truly sorry. I turned my phone off while I was in the meeting with your father and forgot to turn it back on. He suggested, I get an engagement ring for you, so when I left the office, I visited a few jewelry stores."

Her mood picked up at the mention of an engagement ring. "You got me a ring?"

"Two, really. An engagement and wedding ring. And I got you a bracelet to wrap around your pretty wrist."

She bounced around on the couch and stuck her hand out. "Well don't keep me in suspense." Her fingers began to wiggle. "Let's see it?"

He handed the ring box to her. She opened it and her eyes immediately widened. "Oh, Jamie Lee, this is stunning." She glanced up at him. "How did you—?"

"I didn't, I charged it to Soldiers of the Lord."

"Well, it's gorgeous." She put the five-caret diamond engagement ring on her left hand and wriggled her fingers. "How does it look?"

"It looks like it was made for you."

She stood up and hugged him. "Thank you, I feel guilty. I started having bad thoughts and you were buying me a ring."

"And a bracelet. He handed the bracelet box to her. "This is for you, too."

She sat back on the couch and rapidly opened it, reacting much the same as she had with the engagement ring. "Oh, Jamie Lee, it's beautiful." She slipped it on her right wrist and displayed it to her generous fiancé. "It's gorgeous isn't it?"

"It is, but nothing is as gorgeous as you." Jamie Lee felt guilty for deceiving her, but it was necessary. He knew she'd never understand his need for other women, when she was so perfect herself. He didn't even understand it.

She reached her hands around his rear end and pulled him between her legs until his legs bumped the cushion. She brought her elegant long fingered hands around to the front of his slacks and lowered the zipper. "Now, I'm going to give you a reward."

At first, it seemed like a good idea, but then he remembered his manhood had been in Gwen for the better part of two hours and would most likely smell of

The Televangelist I

her sex. As she pulled his flaccid penis out, he stayed her hand. "Sounds like fun, but first I want to taste your first home cooked meal, even if it is dry and overcooked, because I screwed up, and then I want to take a shower so I'm nice and clean for you."

"That sounds like fun. I'll take a shower with you. I love for you to make love to me in the shower."

* * * *

After an energetic round of passion in Sonny's large round bed, he left to make some phone calls in his office. Consuela had never even slept in a round bed, let alone made love in one. She liked having sex in it, and looked forward to sleeping in it. The other thing she liked was mirrors everywhere—behind the bed, beside the bed and above the bed. She couldn't believe how sexy it was to watch—as if part of you were a voyeur spying on the two of you while your partner and you got it on. Lying in the bed, she looked up into the mirror above and fondled herself. It was even sexy watching her playing with herself.

Sitting up, Consuela decided to nose around the reverend's large, sexy bedroom. As Sonny had already demonstrated, no expense had been spared to provide the preacher with the latest in convenience and technological gadgetry. The nearby nightstand contained a specially made control panel, which controlled a large TV screen that lowered from the ceiling. With it, he could also play stereo music at the touch of a button, or if he preferred, watch a movie. If she wanted to see the beautiful night view of Dallas, he could push another button and the motor driven

The Televangelist I

drapes slid aside, exposing the twenty-foot window wall.

Donning one of the reverend's Hugh Hefner style smoking jackets, she headed for the large bookshelf, wondering what kind of books he read. Having seen a bookcase in his office, she assumed these books would be light reading and she was right, seeing titles by Clancy, Demille, Grisham and others.

Noticing the lower portion of the bookcase had doors, she stooped and opened one. It was full of VHS tapes. She pulled one out and examined it. The sleeve featured a photo of a well-endowed, naked woman and was titled, *I Want You*. She slid it back in its space and drew out the adjacent one. This one had two girls and a guy on the cover, in skimpy bathing suits and was called, *Miami Spice*. She put it back and pulled out the next one. More of the same, a side shot of blonde in a bikini bottom only, stooping and holding a naked man. This one was entitled, *Daddy Doesn't Know*. They were *all* porn.

"What do you have there?" Sonny marched up to her and relieved her of the tape.

"Gee Sonny, with all your rabblerousing over the years about porn, I never would have guessed you had a collection of it."

"Don't be naïve. Haven't you noticed that half of the celebrities and politicians caught in a scandal have virulently condemned that very same vice?"

"Now that you mention it—"

"I'll wager fully half of those haranguing against certain vices, be it infidelity, gambling, porn, drugs, prostitutes or homosexuality are caught up in the same vice." He studied the video cassette he'd taken from Consuela. "*Daddy Doesn't Know*. Not a bad flick. Have you ever fucked while someone else is doing the same thing on the screen?"

She frowned. "No, I've missed that experience."

He smiled and pointed at her. "You would like it. Would you like to try it?"

"I guess, if it isn't too demeaning of woman."

He laughed. "Some of it is, isn't it? I have one here where a woman's fantasies are fulfilled. She's treated like a goddess."

"That one I'd like to see."

* * * *

"Don't worry baby. These things happen."

Jamie Lee knew exactly why he couldn't get hard—no matter what Missy tried. It'd only been a few hours ago since he'd fucked Gwen like there was no tomorrow. Add in the fact he'd had sex with Missy at least a half dozen times Saturday and Sunday. Even his enormous virility had limits—he was no sexual superman.

I'll bet I could get hard for that cunt, Cheryl.

Missy, who hadn't given up, had him in her mouth. "It seems like you're getting a little bit hard baby."

That's it, I can get hard for that bitch 'cause I hate her. No...I don't hate her. I love her.

The Televangelist I

A picture of Tommy fucking her came into his mind. He couldn't see their faces but he knew it was them.

Missy exclaimed. "That's it baby, you're almost hard."

Love her? That's impossible, I barely know her, I'm pissed because she wouldn't fuck me and now she's fucking Tommy.

Suddenly, his vision of the fornicating couple shifted and he could see Cheryl's lovely face. Her beautiful blue eyes widened perceptibly and an alarmed expression formed on her face when she saw him. *"Tommy, what are you doing here? I'm so sorry baby."*

Tommy? Tommy turned his head and looked at him, only it wasn't Tommy. It was he, Jamie Lee Vincent, pounding his pud into Cheryl's precious snatch. *"I'm not sorry, Tommy. She's mine and you should have stayed away."*

"Baby you're hard! What do you want to do?"

"Get on the bed any way you want. I just want to slam my cock into your warm slit."

Missy laid on the on the bed and spread her legs.

Jamie Lee, still in a dream state, mounted her and slipped his hunger into her warm, womanly lair.

"Why, Jamie Lee? You could have any girl you want. You already have Missy and Gwen?"

As Tommy watched. I slammed Cheryl with everything I had. She winced in obvious pleasure-pain. I looked up at Tommy's agonized face and reminded him, "You forgot Mother."

Chapter Twelve – Consuela

And, these Islamic fundamentalists, these radical terrorists, these Middle Eastern monsters are committed to destroying the Jewish nation, driving her into the Mediterranean, conquering the world. Rev. Jerry Falwell

Sitting in his office, Jamie Lee received a call on his direct line. "Hello?"

"Hi sweetheart, it's Mom."

"Mom! How did you get my private number?"

"Reverend Riverton gave it to me. He came by and asked me questions about you. We've stayed in contact. Is that a problem?"

Contact? Jamie Lee shook off sudden carnal suspicions. "No, of course not. Sorry, I've been meaning to call you. It's just that I've been so busy."

"I understand. I know what's been happening to you. Reverend Riverton explained it to me, so I understand. I saw you on TV, too. You were sensational, and that girl you're engaged to...I think she's the most beautiful girl I've ever seen and so vivacious."

"Yes, she is, but what's been happening to me is no excuse. I should have come to see you. I'll tell you what. We're shooting seven new shows starting this

Friday, so I'll be busy all week, but this weekend, I'll bring Missy and we'll come to see you."

"Ah, that's sweet of you, but that's not why I called. I've undergone some changes of my own. I've moved to Dallas. Since I'm going to be all alone, I traded the house for a high rise condominium in downtown Dallas."

This took Jamie Lee by surprise. "That's great Mom. What about the store?"

"The trade included exchanging my store for an antique store in Dallas."

"Hmm, that was fortunate."

"Yes, it was. Maybe, some of your good fortune is rubbing off on me. Anyway, they're moving the furniture in today, so I should be organized enough to cook for you and your beautiful lady this Thursday."

"That would be nice. What's your address?"

"Thirty-five oh five Turtle Creek Boulevard, number twelve-oh-six. Oh, and my new phone number is 972-555-4778."

"All right, let met check with Missy. I'll let you know before Thursday."

"Good. I know you're a busy man, so I'll let you go. I love you."

"I love you too, Mom."

* * * *

Surprised to see Tommy home so early Cheryl ran up, embraced and kissed him. Even with his flaws, Tommy was a good man and the love of her life. When their kiss ended, she inquired, "How come you're home so soon?"

The Televangelist I

Tommy pursed his lips to the side. It was clear something was wrong.

"What?"

He shrugged. "I guess he felt sorry fer me."

Cheryl frowned. "I don't understand."

Tommy wouldn't look at her. "I got two weeks' notice, today. They said that with the economy being down and cable TV eating into the stations revenue, they have to tighten their belts. That's why they're laying off ten percent of the work force. It's last hired, first fired and I was dead last."

Cheryl's stomach lurched. It felt as if it'd turned upside down. Unless Tommy could find another job, the only income they would have would be unemployment insurance. She pulled Tommy into her arms. "We'll be all right baby. I'm sure you'll find a new job and if you don't, I'll see what I can find when my classes are over."

"That'd be at night. Where would you work at night?"

She raised her hand a couple feet and slapped them against her thighs. "I don't know yet. This just happened. I do know our neighbor three apartments down is a bartender and he said if I ever needed a job, he could get me in there."

Tommy finally looked at her. "I don't know him. When did you meet him?"

"A couple weeks ago, down by the pool."

"You went down by the pool in that tiny bikini without me and talked with a man?"

The Televangelist I

What does he think I'm going to do? "Yeah. If it bothers you I won't do it anymore."

"It bothers me."

She was annoyed, but decided this was not the time to voice it. "Fine, I won't do it anymore. Just don't blame me for wanting to help."

* * * *

When Jamie Lee and Missy arrived at his Mother's, he was surprised and irritated to find another guest—Sonny Riverton.

With an arm around Missy, Jamie Lee introduced her to his mother. "Missy, this is my mother, Consuela Vincent."

Consuela grasped Missy's hands. "I've been dying to meet you. You are so beautiful." She leaned in and kissed her on the cheek.

"Oh, thank you, Consuela. It's my pleasure, really."

"Connie, please." She winked.

"If you insist." Missy turned to Jamie Lee, obviously confused. "How can this be? She looks like your older sister, not your mother."

Consuela scoffed at Missy's flattery. "Oh, Missy, not everyone falls apart when they hit thirty-five."

"How old are you?" Missy blurted out, most likely without thinking.

Consuela leaned in and whispered, "It's our secret, I'm going to be forty-one soon."

Not really having a mother she could relate to, Missy gravitated to her future mother-in-law, and the two seemed inseparable through dinner and

The Televangelist I

afterwards. Although Jamie Lee and Sonny were occasionally joined the conversation, they were mostly fended for themselves. After dinner, they adjourned to the living room, where Consuela served dessert with coffee and brandy.

Jamie Lee believed the reverend's mere presence signaled that his mother and future father-in-law had begun a relationship. The fact that the reverend couldn't seem to keep his eyes of her and she would occasionally cast furtive glances at him only confirmed it. Despite his slow burn, Jamie Lee held his temper in check and played with the cards he'd been dealt, acting warm and friendly to the reverend. "What did you think of the audience last week, Boss?"

"I thought they were great. You never know about the television audience until they air. Tomorrow should be a test for you to see if there's any second guessing about your birthright."

"Tell me Sonny, can you tell when you have the audience in the palm of your hand?"

He smiled. "Oh yes, I can feel it—a oneness with the audience."

"Yes, that's it, a oneness. That's what I felt last week when I went out there."

"Son, I've been watching you. You have the potential to be one of the best, if not the best, ever."

And I don't even believe in God.

Jamie Lee's burgeoning ego was not above flattery and he reveled in any praise he received, but he especially gloried in compliments from his mentor — the reverend. "You really think so?"

The Televangelist I

"Son, I studied them all from Graham and Roberts to Copeland and you have the potential to top them all."

Somewhat calmed, Jamie Lee discussed the ins and outs of his new career with Sonny until nine-thirty, when he announced he was tired and it was time for them to leave.

* * * *

Driving home in Missy's BMW—Jamie Lee hadn't taken delivery of his new Mercedes yet—Missy seemed ecstatic. "You know I'd always heard horror stories about mother-in-laws, but I just love your mother."

Paying more attention to the road than Jamie Lee, she didn't see him roll his eyes. "Yeah, she can be nice."

The sarcasm was thick, as she replied, "You sound really enthusiastic. Did you know my father has a penthouse in the same building? I'll bet they're seeing each other."

Jamie Lee bet so too, but that's not what Jamie Lee wanted to hear. "I hope not."

"Why, they make a darling couple, even with my father being eighteen years older. Your mother looks so good."

"Yeah, she's always been a looker."

"Has she ever been married?"

"Ah-huh, she married a guy, I don't remember, shortly after I was born. Probably, so I'd have a father. She kicked him out after a couple of years, but not before he fathered my sister Lindsay, who died of pneumonia when I was seven."

"Oh, Jamie Lee, I'm so sorry."

"Don't worry about it. I was so young, I barely remember her."

* * * *

Sonny wrapped his arms around Connie as she finished undressing in his bedroom. "What did you think, baby?"

"I thought it went fairly well. I could tell he strongly suspects we're seeing each other, but he's in no position to do anything about it and knows it."

As Sonny removed the last of his clothes and joined her under the covers, he sidled up beside her and began to nibble on one of her stiff nipples.

"Mmm. That feels good baby." Her fingers tunneled through his long salt and pepper hair. "Sonny?"

"Yes, Honey?"

"Is Jamie Lee as good as you say?"

He answered with her nipple in his mouth, "Uh-huh," and pushed a digit between her legs.

"I hate to stop you, but I asked to come into your bed so we could watch one of your wicked movies."

He pulled away and laughed. "Liked that, did you?"

She raised her eyebrows and smiled. "I never had five climaxes before."

Sonny rolled out of bed. "What do you feel like, my sweet?"

Her smile turned coy. "Do you have something where the lucky lady is serviced by two or more studs?"

The Televangelist I

He chuckled, "Like you were at Monterey?"

Her stare became reprimanding. "That's not funny."

"Sorry"

"But yes, like that, but not one at a time. I'd like to see the girl enjoy and work all the men at the same time."

He stooped at his bookcase and perused the titles. He pulled a tape out and rose. "Here we go. Three on one. How does that sound?"

She watched as he strode to the VCR. "Promising."

He bent down and slid the tape in the slot. "Do you ever think of that night?"

"Sometimes, and surprisingly, not with revulsion."

Pushing the play button, he turned the TV on and made sure the movie had started, before slipping between the sheets and Connie's waiting arms. "That's not surprising. You ended up with a fine young man."

And lover. "That's true, but in hindsight I also find it to be an exhilarating memory."

She smirked as Sonny's eyes widened. "Sweetheart, do you think we could start tonight with your talented tongue down below. I'd like to see how many releases you could give me in one night."

The Televangelist I

Chapter Thirteen - Danielle

Lord, give us righteous judges who will not try to legislate and dominate this society. Take control, Lord! We ask for additional vacancies on the court. –
Rev. Pat Robertson

Jamie Lee and Missy arrived at the studio by one-thirty. The ever-confident Jamie Lee was nervous for some reason and he didn't know why. After getting made-up and dressed, he met Missy, who looked ravishing in her floor length ball gown, backstage.

Together, they watched the audience enter and settle in, while Sonny eased up behind them and placed an arm on each of their shoulders. "How's it look?"

Jamie Lee and Missy both looked at the reverend. "Looks pretty good, Daddy."

Sonny squeezed Jamie Lee's shoulder. "How 'bout you son? How are you doing?"

He tittered. "I'm more nervous than the first time."

"We've slated a little champagne and caviar get-together for the media after the taping, so stick around."

"How come, sir?"

"I figured it's time the news people get to know our new star. I told the media people you would be available for questions. Is that all right?"

He shrugged. "I'd have to do it sooner or later. I hope I don't screw up."

Sonny laughed. "Don't worry son. You're a natural."

The director came over and whispered in Sonny's ear.

"I gotta go." He walked away, and then partially angled back toward Jamie Lee. "Son, you'll be fine once you get out there."

Jamie Lee watched and waited as the reverend warmed the crowd up with charisma and a little self-deprecating humor. He was good, no doubt about it.

After five minutes, he introduced and waved for Missy. The audience loved her and why shouldn't they? She was beautiful effervescent and ostensibly pure. Every woman dreamed about having a daughter like her and every man longed for a wife like her, but she belonged to him.

What is wrong with me? Why is the woman every man dreams of not good enough? Is any conquest, any success good enough.

Jamie Lee honestly wanted to be like everyone else. He wanted to love and feel things for others, but it seemed beyond him. His reverie was interrupted when the reverend introduced and waved for him.

The reverend held out his hand and winked. "I know you all have been waiting for our new wonder

The Televangelist I

boy, so without further adieu here is *Jamie Lee...
Vincent!*

Jamie Lee's worries and nervousness morphed
into a giant smile when the crowd stood and went
berserk. He laughed as signs like, WE LOVE OUR
BASTARD! and DA VINCI AND QUEEN ELIZABETH
ARE BASTARDS TOO! were raised up high. Waving
and throwing kisses, he sauntered out, flashing his
winsome smile and nodding his head in mini bows. As
he took the mic from Sonny, the crowd broke into a
chant...Bastard...Bastard...Bastard! Jamie Lee knew
from that moment on, he would never have to regret
not knowing his father, because, religion and Sonny
Riverton had made his illegitimate birth status a non
sequitur.

After the crowd calmed down, Jamie Lee said, "I
want to thank everyone for the warm welcome."

There was a smattering of applause, but he
quickly raised a hand. Then Jamie Lee began to bounce
on the balls of his feet. "You know why I'm bouncing?"

"No," The audience said unanimously.

"I'm bouncing because I feel the Lords energy
tingling through my body. I feel the Lord with us
today. It's especially strong right now. Ooh, it is so
strong! Can you feel him?"

Various affirmative answers issued out among the
audience.

He pointed his forefinger up and out. "You know
why his presence is so strong right here, right now,
today?"

"No!"

The Televangelist I

Jamie smiled and wiped his brow. "Two reasons. One is he loves each and every one of us and two is, he wants to check up on his latest gamble — me!"

Laughter filtered from the crowd.

"You laugh, but I was a gamble. I was lost. I was a sinner and yet God forgave me and wiped away my sins. That is the beauty of God. You don't have to fill out an application. You don't have to have a credit check. All God wants, is for you to say, 'take me God. I'm all yours,' and your life starts over."

More scattered clapping

"It's hard not to sin. God knows that. How many of you sinned today?"

A few hands went up.

"That's all? I sinned today. I called a certain politician, whom I won't name, a son-of-a-bitch."

Laughter.

"You know, Lying by omission is a sin too. Now tell me, how many of you sinned this week?"

Almost all hands went up.

He smiled. Now we're getting somewhere.

More laughter.

"The good news is our God is a loving and forgiving God. I'm not going to go to hell for calling somebody a bad name and unless you are an unrepentant axe murderer, you're not going for your sins either."

Jamie Lee continued his sermon for another four minutes, after which he received a standing ovation, Bastard chants and all.

The Televangelist I

After the show, at the media get-together, Jamie Lee was the center of attention. As expected, he fielded questions from an assemblage of media guests for several minutes. What he didn't expect, was to be wildly attracted to one of his questioners. She was a tall, svelte, cat-like creature with huge, brown eyes and long, black hair in a black and white, polka dot, summer dress. He couldn't take his eyes off her.

With everyone trying to ask questions, she mostly listened, but when she did ask a question, it was incisive and pertinent. All through the question and answer session, she stared at him. He found her penetrating gaze and Mona Lisa smile unsettling, as if she knew something the others didn't—that even *he* didn't.

Then, when one of the others asked a cumbersome and complicated question, she vanished. He looked for, but couldn't spot her. After a dozen more questions the reporters slipped away, and he was free to search for the mystery woman, but she'd apparently left.

He spotted Missy and Sonny talking with some potential advertisers—much too boring for him. He headed to the buffet table to grab a plastic flute of Dom Perignon and caviar. He set the champagne down and began to spread beluga on crackers.

"I must say you seemed better than last week," a sultry voice said to his left.

He angled his head. It was *her*. He turned and smiled. "You really think so?"

"Oh yes, you seemed much more in control." She offered her white gloved hand and flashed a very white, friendly smile. "Hi, I'm Danny."

Taking her hand, he chuckled. "You don't look like any Danny I ever met."

Her smile turned coquettish. "I try to represent my gender favorably."

He arched his eyebrows. "I would say more like magnificently."

"Why thank you. That's one of the nicest compliments I've ever received.
It makes me feel guilty, for not telling you how handsome you are, but I'm sure you are sick to death of hearing it."

He couldn't help but laugh. This woman fascinated him, but he had to be careful, Missy had glanced his way. "Is that right? Let me ask you, do you get tired of hearing how absolutely stunning you are?"

She shook her head, her long hair trailing behind. "No, I never get tired of hearing it. Of course, you are the first person who's put it quite like that. Why don't you let me interview you and you could tell me that between each question?"

He grinned at her dry humor. "I'll think about it."

"You do that." She slipped a card in his hand. "Meanwhile, I have to run. I have a date." She winked. "And I'll bet he won't tell me how absolutely stunning I am." She batted her eyelashes. "Call me."

His eyes followed as her superbly crafted legs sashayed across the room toward the exit. Missy watched her too, and then she looked at him. He slid

The Televangelist I

the card in his jacket pocket, plastered a smile on his lips and headed toward his *absolutely stunning* fiancé.

But Missy wasn't smiling. "I hope you gave that *bitch* a piece of your mind."

Jamie Lee frowned in confusion. "No. Should I have?"

"I think so. She didn't write very nice things about you last week."

His frown deepened. "Really, who is it?"

"That's Danielle White."

His eyes went for narrow to wide. He pulled out the card and glanced at it.

'Danielle (Danny) White, Society and Religion Editorialist.'

He winced. Nevertheless, he surreptitiously slipped it back into his pocket. After all, she asked him to call.

* * * *

The following Monday, after his second show appeared on TV, Jamie Lee made a point of picking up a copy of *The Fort Worth Star Telegram*.

As he exited the elevator, he barely acknowledged Gwen. "Hi Doll, would you bring me an orange juice."

Spreading the paper out on his desk, he skipped to the religious section anxious to see what Danny White had to say about his performance.

This time, above the byline of Danielle White, the headline blazed, '**Bastard Preacher Woo's Fans and Me**,' this article had a markedly different tone. Starting

The Televangelist I

with, "In his sophomore effort Sunday, 'Soldiers of the Lord,' phenom—self-proclaimed bastard, Jamie Lee Vincent, mesmerized the audience and took a big step toward winning me over. This talented and charismatic new pastor at least gained my respect when following the show I had the pleasure of meeting him. He never brought up the mostly negative article I'd written about him on his initial outing. Instead, he chose to focus on the positive and let me tell you, this man can be positive-ly charming.

"At this point I'm on the fence as to Jamie Lee Vincent's future. He could become the greatest preacher since Billy Graham or like Humpty Dumpty fall off and never be heard from again. Let's face it; the world loves and underdog, and I do too. I'm betting on the former. Go Jamie Lee, you bastard!

The article tickled Jamie Lee's funny bone. He loved it. At first, he dug Danny's card out to call her, then decided it wasn't personal enough. Jamie walked into the reception area with the paper under his arm. Gwen, I'm going for an early lunch.

Jamie Lee drove to Every Blooming Thing, the florist SOL used exclusively and charged three dozen white and red mixed roses on the ministries account. As an afterthought, he also sent a dozen red roses each to Gwen and Missy.

It was a beautiful summery day, so when Jamie came out of the florist, he set the top of his expensive new car down. The drive to the Fort Worth Star Telegram was about twenty-five miles. When he

The Televangelist I

arrived, he managed to find a parking space right on Seventh Street. After filling the parking meter with enough coins to reach the two-hour limit, he walked into the reception area, flowers and all. He walked up to the receptionist and asked directions, "Could you direct me to the office of Danielle White?"

"Do you have an appointment?"

"No, this is just a spontaneous visit."

The lady smiled. "Tell me your name and I'll call her."

"Couldn't you just direct me?"

"No. We have a policy where every visitor has to have an escort. In your case it would be Mrs. White."

"Mrs.?"

"Yes, Mrs. White."

Jamie was confused and remembering the last thing she said, *"Meanwhile, I have to run. I have a date. And I'll bet he won't tell me how absolutely stunning I am. Call me."* with good reason.

"I'll tell you what. Just see she gets these. Will you?"

* * * *

Jamie Lee hadn't been back five minutes when Gwen called him on the intercom. "While you were gone, Ms White called."

A shot of adrenalin ran through Jamie Lee's veins. "Thank you Gwen."

"You want her number?"

"I have it, thank you."

As soon as Gwen was off the phone, he dialed Danny.

The Televangelist I

"Danielle White. May I help you?"

"Did you get my flowers?"

"Hi! I did, they were stunning."

He laughed

"I take it the incomparable Jamie Lee Vincent approved of my last article."

He chuckled. "He did, in fact he got such a kick out it, he wants to grant you the interview you asked for."

"Fantastic. Oh, but there's a problem. Can his 'wonderfulness', wait a measly four weeks to give me the interview?"

Jamie Lee's brow furrowed. "If he has to, but why?"

"Because, my plane to Los Angeles, leaves tomorrow at ten a.m. to catch the four week South Sea and Far East Cruise I've been waiting to go on for three months."

"South Sea Cruise? I wish I could go with you."

"Ummm, I can picture it now. You and me alone on the beach Pago Pago? Be still my heart."

Jamie Lee snickered. "I can too, you in your tiny bikini, sipping on pina colada's."

"You know it sounds sinful to be on a south sea beach with you and wearing anything."

He laughed. "Why couldn't we do it tonight?"

"Do what? Oh, the interview. We could, but four of my co-workers are sending me off with a bon voyage party tonight at Barneys. You're welcome."

"I would but..."

"Yeah, I know."

The Televangelist I

"I thought you were married?"

"What made you think that?"

"The receptionist at your building emphasized you are a Mrs."

"I was, but I'm not, now. That's part of the reason for the cruise."

He smiled. "So tell me. Did your date tell you how absolutely stunning you are?"

"What? Oh that. No, I knew he wouldn't. I'll tell you about it when we do the interview. Can I call you when I get back?"

"Please do."

"Alright, I'm really looking forward to getting to know the real you. Bye."

"Me too. Good-bye. Have a fun trip."

"Thanks."

The Televangelist I

Chapter Fourteen – Michael
*AIDS is not just God's punishment for homosexuals;
it is God's punishment for the society that tolerates
homosexuals.* Rev. Jerry Falwell

Five weeks Later

The reverend's intercom rang. He pushed the speaker button. "Yes, Gwen?"

"You have a phone call on line one from a Larry Miller. It might be a salesman. Would you like me to get rid of him?"

"Please."

"Yes sir, just a second." She switched to the other line for few seconds, and then came back on. "Sir, he's quite insistent."

"Ask him what he wants?"

Once again, she put him on hold. "He says he's been reading about Jamie Lee in the papers and doesn't like what he's reading."

Larry Miller...hmm...Larry Miller. Who could that be? Then it struck him, Lawrence Miller—*Rance!* "Gwen, put Mr. Miller through."

* * * *

The day before their wedding engagement show, Jamie received a call from his mother that Sonny needed to see Missy and him as soon as possible. When they arrived, his mother answered the door, but understood as soon as he saw the reverend.

They stepped in and the first thing Jamie Lee saw was Sonny, a dazed look in his reddish eyes, sitting on the couch in a smoking jacket and slippers, blubbering. He held a glass of amber liquid in his hand and a half empty bottle of Wild Turkey rested on the cocktail table.

Missy sensed what happened before a word was exchanged. She screamed, "Oh, dear God. No! You can't have my brother!" and weeping uncontrollably, ran to her Daddy. They both hugged and cried.

Jamie Lee even felt sorry for them. He looked at Sonny hoping to get an explanation, but he was in no condition for conversation.

Instead, Connie explained what happened, "Sonny received a call, this morning, from Loving Rest convalescence home. Michael had tried to kill himself, and was sent by ambulance to the Baylor University Medical Center in Dallas. Before we even had a chance to get dressed a second call came that he had passed away."

"What do you mean he tried to kill himself?"

She looked confused. "I'm not sure baby, the word I got was he shoved a spoon down his throat and choked to death on it."

Jamie Lee cringed. "Ooh! That sounds awful." He poured himself a third of a glass of the bourbon and swallowed it.

Connie went on, "Under the circumstances the engagement show will have to be postponed. The funeral will be in two days. The engagement can be announced a week or so later."

Sonny held out the empty bottle to Connie. "Ran out."

She took the bottle and went to the dining room table, which held a case of the bourbon and grabbed a new bottle. She also went in the powder room and returned with a box of Kleenex, since Missy and her father had used all the tissues up. Taking her seat, she handed Missy a tissue and Sonny a full glass of Wild Turkey. She then joined in, embracing and commiserating with the two of them.

Jamie Lee filled his glass from the fresh bottle of bourbon mom had brought and sat across from them in one of the occasional chairs. The two of them were miserable and it was depressing. He filled his glass again and again. Soon he grew restless. "How about if I go out and get a pizza?"

Missy stopped sobbing long enough to say, "I'm not hungry, but you go ahead."

By the time Jamie Lee returned with two extra large pizzas, one plain and one pepperoni, Bobbi Sue and Grant had arrived. Bobbi Sue was torn up too, but more in control than Missy. She took one piece of plain pizza, as did Jamie Lee's mom. Grant and he sat at the dining room table eating several slices of pepperoni pizza.

While they sat there, Grant told Jamie Lee, he and Bobbi Sue had been at the funeral home making arrangements. He hadn't realized Bobbi Sue could be that helpful. It was good to see one family member stand up and take care of things, because Sonny and Missy sure weren't in any condition to do anything.

Jamie Lee rose to get a soda. "When and where is it?"

"After they get the body, it'll be prepared, at the Logan Brother's funeral home. Following that, Michael will be available for viewing at our church sanctuary until the actual funeral, which will commence Saturday at eleven a.m.

"Bobbi Sue and I don't know if Sonny will be in any condition to do the eulogy. We have enlisted a couple of Michael's friends to say something, but we both hoped you would deliver a eulogy." Jamie Lee watched a tear roll down from one of Grant eyes. After swiping at it with the side of his hand he continued, "He liked you, you know. He knew, being gay, he could never take Sonny's place, so he thought and hoped you might be the straight son Sonny deserved. Will you do it? I know you could do a damned good job."

What could Jamie Lee say? He nodded and Grant told everyone Jamie Lee was going to deliver the eulogy.

They all agreed it was a good idea. Missy came up to him and kissed him. "Thank you baby. I know you didn't know him very well, so I'll help you write it." She picked up a piece of pizza and took a bite and then another. When she finished, she said, "I'm doing better now. I didn't realize how hungry I was." After eating a second piece, she added, "I want to go now, so we can work on Michael's eulogy. It's very important to me."

The Televangelist I

* * * *

Cheryl walked into the living room and Tommy glanced up from the TV. "What are you doin' all fixed up?"

Wearing jeans and a blouse, she wasn't really fixed up. She just had a lot of make-up on. "I'm off to work. Wish me luck. I'm nervous."

Tommy's brow furrowed. "Work where?"

"Jack got me the job at the bar where he works. You haven't had any luck finding work and we're out of money. You only get two-hundred and thirty-five dollars a week. The bills are overdue, the power is going to be shut off and the rent alone eats up your unemployment check. I need to contribute."

"I've been looking. Every day I go out searching for work. I could work in Louisiana, but you don't want me to."

"I know you do. We've only been married two-and-a-half months and I don't want us to be apart. I'll just do this until you find work. Give me a kiss, I have to go."

"Whoa! Wait a minute." Tommy rose. "What's dis place called? Where is it?"

She'd hoped to avoid this. Reluctantly, she answered. "It's called Babes Galore. It's near the airport."

An incredulous look formed on his face. "Dat's a strip joint?"

"Topless. But I'm just going to be a waitress. No stage, no topless. Let me just try this for week and if the money isn't that good you can take that job in Louisiana."

Tears welled in his eyes. "Dis isn't fair. I love you, want to support you and can't. Go, but I'll be stopping by, so you better not be on stage, topless."

"I won't." She edged up to him. "I'm late, gimmie a kiss and wish me luck."

They kissed lightly. "Luck."

* * * *

It seemed like he'd barely fallen asleep when he felt Cheryl slid in bed and ease up to him. She wrapped an arm around him, kissed his chest and neck and squeezed his manhood hard. "Are you asleep?" She whispered, "I'm horny as a bitch in heat."

That was the only invitation Tommy needed.

When they finished. Tommy looked at the clock. It read 3:45 am. With her still in his arms he thered ask, "How'd it go?"

She kissed him and grabbed him again. "Baby, I made a hundred and seventy-four."

"Wow. That's more dan I made when I worked. You want ta go again?"

"Ah-huh. That atmosphere made me feel frisky. Can you? Is it all right?"

This time Cheryl straddled his hips and rode his joystick, cowgirl style.

They were still at it when the sun rose and Cheryl slept through her Composition and Rhetoric class that day.

* * * *

The Televangelist I

If the guest book could be a guide, over a thousand people visited Michael as he reposed for open casket viewing in the sanctuary that Friday.

Saturday, the day of the funeral was hectic. All Riverton family members gathered in the church mess hall for coffee and sweet rolls, while guests traipsed into the mega cathedral, which claimed to hold ten thousand. When eleven o'clock came, the family entered the main hall through the sanctuary and except for Reverend Riverton, took their seats in the front row.

Jamie Lee stared out over the throng. There was a substantially larger audience than the five hundred which the studio held. His mom was in the third row and the bright red hair of Gwen stood out a row behind and to the right of her. His eyes darted back to a spot he'd scanned. He couldn't be sure, but with her long, sandy blonde hair, it looked like...the *bitch*...Cheryl. And seated next to her was her lap dog, Tommy.

It was them all right and when this was over, he planned to seek them out and talk with them.

Just then, he heard the reverend say. "Everyone, please be seated. We are about to begin."

Jamie Lee took his seat, next to Missy. Since they would soon be announcing their engagement, it was deemed all right for them to be seen together.

Sonny stood at the lectern on the pulpit thumbing through what was most likely a bible. He didn't look good. He looked sallow and gaunt, a shadow of the powerful presence, which had coerced him that night, in Missy's motor home, to commit to marriage.

The Televangelist I

The reverend looked up. "Dearly beloved. We are gathered here to celebrate the life and honor the passing of Michael Robert Riverton...my son. I have presided over hundreds of funerals over the years and this...is the hardest thing I've ever had to do. A mother or father should never have to suffer the loss of their offspring, yet it happened to me and I...as his and your pastor, am obligated to preside over his funeral. He..."

The reverend stopped and turned away from the lectern. When he turned back, he waved for Jamie Lee to join him. Jamie Lee joined him and ignoring the crowd, they conferred, "Jamie Lee, I can't do this. Could you take over?"

"I would be honored, sir."

"Good." Sonny turned back to the lectern. "I thought I could force myself to do this, but, forgive me, I am too overwrought. I hope you don't mind, but I'm turning this proceeding over to my future son-in-law, Jamie Lee Vincent."

To a man, woman and child the assembly rose and applauded for sixty seconds. Whether they applauded in understanding for the reverend's feelings or for the rising star about to take over, no one will ever know. Perhaps, a little of both.

Jamie Lee captivated the audience with his sermon. After speaking for fifteen minutes, he introduced a half dozen friends or associates who said nice things and told funny stories about Michael. Since Jamie Lee had taken over for the reverend, Missy delivered a rousing eulogy. When she finished, her fiancé took over and closed the proceeding.

The Televangelist I

"That finishes the service. For those of you who have not viewed Michael and wish to, we will allow you thirty minutes to do so. Because you are so numerous, please form two lines and move quickly."

As two lines began to form, Jamie Lee continued. "Everyone is invited to join us at the cemetery for the short interment ceremony. That will take place at the Logan Brothers Funeral Home and Cemetery in approximately one hour. If you wish to attend, we will leave together in forty-five minutes for the trip there. With the help of patrolmen, we hope to have an orderly procession."

By the time he went to speak with Cheryl and Tommy, it was too late. They had slipped out.

The procession to the cemetery had so many cars and was so long, the four-mile trip took thirty minutes. The service was held at the family tomb. Cameras, which had been banned at the cathedral, were allowed at the cemetery in force, including the media.

As promised, the service was a short five minutes. Reporters tried unsuccessfully to collar the reverend, Jamie Lee and other family members. One of them did manage to ask Missy about the reverend's future son-in-law comment, to which she replied, "If you wait a week or so you'll see."

For that reporter and all within earshot, that was confirmation and the headline in *The Dallas Morning News* the next day read — Missy to Marry Bastard Preacher — while *The Fort Worth Star Telegraph* had a slightly different take—Jamie Lee to Join the Riverton Clan.

* * * *

The reverend didn't come into the office until the following Thursday.

About an hour later, Mike Hennings walked past Gwen and walked into the Reverend's office. "You want to see me boss?"

Sonny looked up. "Yes, hi Mike. I have another job for you. Have a seat."

Gwen brought his usual cup of black coffee and handed it to him. Edging the chair closer to the bosses desk he set his coffee down and propped his feet up next to the coffee cup. Sonny almost said something, but he bit his tongue.

Before we get started, I want to let you know how sorry we all are for your loss. Tragic!"

"Thank you. I appreciate it."

"No problem. Now, what you got, boss?"

"The day before Michael died, I heard from Lawrence Miller."

Hennings frowned. "Who?"

Sonny chuckled, "Same thing I said. The one we decided was Jamie Lee's father, remember."

Hennings lowered his feet and took a sip of coffee. "Oh yeah. The commune leader, Rance." He laughed. "My how the mighty have fallen? What did Rance want?"

With a touch of sarcasm, the reverend blurted out, "Only a hundred thousand, a year."

The Televangelist I

Mike gulped. "Greedy son of a bitch. What do you want done?"

"Well, let me explain what's at stake and then you decide. We have set Jamie Lee up to be my co-pastor at a minimum and the new Soldiers of the Lord leader, when I decide to call it quits. In those positions, Jamie Lee would make the consortium hundreds of millions of dollars. Obviously, we could afford to pay the appliance salesman from Racine, Wisconsin, but the way I see it, we could never be sure Rance, wouldn't sell us out to a higher bidder."

"A higher bidder like who, what?"

"A magazine, a book deal. Jamie Lee is going to be fair game, that's why we had to work the kinks out of his history."

"What about the fact he raped Jamie Lee's mother. Couldn't we threaten to file a complaint against him?"

"I don't know. I'm just an ole preacher from Lubbock, Texas. That's your bailiwick. Is there a statute of limitations in California, where the crime took place? And if a rape complaint could still be filed after twenty-one years, can he be extradited?"

"You know Sonny. I don't know. We have some people who do though. Let me check the options and I'll proceed." Hennings stood. "Don't worry, I'll take care of everything. Oh, I have a question."

Sonny raised his eyebrows and waited for him to continue.

"That hot red head out there. Does she belong to anyone?"

Sonny smiled. "What do you think?"

Hennings grinned. "I should have known, you dirty old man."

About three minutes after Hennings left Gwen rushed in looking upset. "I have a complaint. Sort of. Did you tell that man, I was your private stock?"
"No, I let him assume you were. Why, do you like him?"
"He makes my skin crawl."
"Then you better let him think you're my private stock."

When Jamie Lee arrived at the office that day, he stopped to say hi to Gwen. "Good morning gorgeous."
"Good morning lover."
Jamie Lee raised his forefinger to his lips. "Shoosh. We don't want to let the pussy out of the bag."
She giggled. "You're so funny."
"I don't suppose Sonny is in."
"As a matter of fact he is. He's taking care of a few things before he takes off for a few days." She waggled her pretty reddish brown eyebrows. "You know what that means."
"Do I ever. We'll talk about that later. Right now I want to catch him while he's in."
The reverend looked up when Jamie Lee opened the door and stepped in. "Good morning Jamie Lee. Thanks for bailing me out Sunday."

The Televangelist I

Jamie Lee took his usual seat opposite the big man and waved off the thanks. "Auf, it was nothing really. It's my job."

"Well thanks anyway. I was fortunate you were there to save me from a very embarrassing moment."

"Thanks are not necessary."

"Well thanks just the same. Michael's death took a lot out of me. The only reason I came in today was to get ready for the show tomorrow. We have to get the engagement over with." He looked up and smiled. "Are you ready to propose in front of ten million viewers?"

"I am."

"Good. Now, what can I do for you?"

"I wondered if you knew the name of a good investigator."

"Why?"

He flexed his brow and shrugged. "I saw an old friend, whom I'd lost track of, at the funeral service and I want to find out where he lives and what he's doing. I may even ask him to be my best man."

Sonny chuckled. "Son, I have just the person for you. In fact you just missed him." He scribbled a name and number on a scratch pad, ripped off the top page and handed it to Jamie Lee. "His name is Michael Hennings and he's done a lot of work for us."

"Thanks, just what I needed."

"Think nothing of it. By the way, I won't be in next week so you'll be in charge."

"Oh."

The Televangelist I

"Ah-huh. Right after the show tomorrow, Connie's taking me to Vegas for some R & R."

A cold chill surged through Jamie Lee. His eyes opened wide and he stared unblinking at the reverend.

Sonny's eyelids narrowed "You are aware your mother and I are seeing each other?"

Jamie Lee's lips quivered as he forced, "I figured."

Sonny leaned forward, elbows on his desk. "You don't have a problem with that, do you?"

Jamie Lee's mind flashed back six years, when one of his mother's *man* friends left after spending the night.

"Why do you do it Mom?"

"Sometimes, I just need the company of a man."

"I'm a man."

She laughed. "You're a boy."

"No, I'm not, I'm a man and when you're with a man I hear you, and it makes me hard." He opened the fly of his pajamas and showed her. "Even in your night gown, you make me hard."

She blinked. "Oh my, I hadn't noticed." Her fingers wrapped around it and squeezed. "You are a man!"

"Son!"

Jamie Lee returned to the present. "Yes sir."

"You looked like you were in never-never land. I asked you a question."

"Yes, sir. My Mom and I are close and I am very protective of her, but if she's going to have a man friend, I couldn't think of a better one than you."

Sonny smiled. "Good. I appreciate that you and she are so close, but you needn't worry. My intentions

The Televangelist I

are as honorable toward her as yours are toward my Missy."

The next day, Jamie Lee's proposal to Missy was telecast live from the studio.

* * * *

Tommy plopped down on the couch beside Cheryl. "What're you watching?"

"Quiet, I want to hear this. Jamie Lee is about to propose."

"All right! Way to go Jamie Lee!"

Cheryl elbowed him then, fascinated, her gaze returned to the TV screen. She had to admit they made a striking couple. Jamie Lee always was handsome. That's why she went out with him.

He stood, wearing a white tuxedo with a ruffled white shirt and a lilac cummerbund. Seated before him on an ornate chair, the lovely and graceful Missy Riverton wore a white ball gown with lilac flowers the color of which matched his cummerbund. As he knelt before her, he took her gloved hand and kissed it. "Missy Riverton, my love, if God were to grant me a single wish, there is nothing in the entire universe, be it fame, wealth or life eternal, that I would pick over you. Will you make my dreams come true and become my wife?"

Missy waited for the applause to die down before responding, "Jamie Lee Vincent, my knight in shining armor, I love you more than life itself. I can think of no greater calling than becoming your wife and I can't wait until we're married."

Cheryl shivered and cringed. "Oh, that poor girl."

The Televangelist I

"Why do you say that?"

She snarled, "Because he's evil."

"You had one bad experience with him and you think he's evil. I hung around with him for years. Yes, sometimes he was a little difficult, but I never thought of him as evil.

"Trust me, he's evil."

"Maybe he's changed. Maybe he even believes in God now."

Cheryl's mouth hung open and to the side. "What? The Bastard Preacher…doesn't believe in God?

"He didn't, but that's what I mean. With all the good things that have happened to him, maybe he's changed his mind."

"A leopard never changes their spots."

"Well, if you hate him so much, why are you watching him?"

"People like him fascinate me. That's why my minor is in Psychology."

Chapter Fifteen – Vegas Honeymoon

You say you're supposed to be nice to the Episcopalians and the Presbyterians and the Methodists and this, that, and the other thing. Nonsense. I don't have to be nice to the spirit of the Antichrist. Rev. Pat Robertson

"My God woman, don't you ever slow down?"

Connie pulled Sonny out of her mouth to answer, "Not, on my honeymoon, I don't."

"Don't forget baby, I'm eighteen years older than you. Can we stop for a few minutes and let me recuperate."

She paused and lay back onto the pillows into Sonny's waiting arm. She kissed his cheek. "All right. I'm sorry; it's just that I waited twenty years to be able to fuck righteously."

He laughed. "Now that's an odd combination of words."

She held her left hand out and admired the rock on her ring finger. "This is the most beautiful ring I have ever seen. Thank you." She kissed his cheek again. I can't believe we did it. I thought you were pulling my leg."

"Yep, I felt guilty divorcing Bernice, but she won't care."

"How did you manage to divorce her so quickly?"

"I actually started the divorce years ago. I just never saw a need to complete it until I met you. With Michael gone plus Bobbi Sue and Missy about to both be married, I needed some stability in my life. I needed someone to talk to and share my largess."

"You're cute. That's why I love you. Not counting Jamie Lee, it took me forty years to find a man to love."

"And you know I love you. I even called my attorney to change my will before we came here?"

"You did?"

"Ah-huh. It was time. With Michael dying and Missy getting married a lot has changed recently, the will needed updating. You never know I might have a heart attack with all this righteous fucking and I wouldn't want anyone contesting your right to your share."

"That's sweet. I never thought of that. Thank you." She giggled. "Jamie Lee is going to be so pissed. I hope he doesn't do anything irrational."

"Really, why would he be angry?"

"Oh, I think you need to use a stronger word than angry. Something more like livid or furious. I hope he doesn't start smashing things"

Sonny shook his head. "I guess I really don't follow."

"I know this is hard to understand, but Jamie Lee thinks of himself as my protector, almost like he is my husband instead of my son."

"That's kind of nutty isn't it?"

"That's what most people would think, but if you think from his perspective it's not so crazy. Remember

The Televangelist I

except for one year, Jamie Lee was fatherless and I was without a husband. He was the de facto man of the house. He thought of himself as my husband and son."

"Still sounds nutty to me." Sonny glanced between his legs. "I think I might be ready for another round."

"Fantastic. I'll tell you what. For the rest of the honeymoon, I'll do all the work and all you have to do his enjoy what I do to you."

* * * *

Cheryl wondered what was up when Syn told her the boss man wanted to see her. "Yes, Mr. Slabova. Syn said you wanted to see me."

"Yes, Cheryl thank you, have a seat. Please."

Cheryl sat in a beat up old chair, knees together.

Joe Slabova, a fortyish man with a receding hairline was an immigrant from Serbia, who spoke good English, but with an accent. He was a big man and kept his office cold and she only had on a skimpy bikini.

She grew uneasy as he stared at her breasts. She knew the cool air had hardened her nipples. Finally, he spoke, "We have a problem. I run a titty bar and the best-looking girl I have won't flash her titties. What am I supposed to do?"

Cheryl didn't like the way the conversation had started, but said nothing.

"Stand up."

She rose, standing as she was taught in modeling school.

"Turn around."

The Televangelist I

She did, standing with one hand on her hip.

"Nice. Great legs and ass. You are prime stuff. Turn back around."

She spun and faced him.

"Gorgeous, just gorgeous. I know you're married and I agreed to let you just wait tables, hoping when you saw what the less attractive girls made, you would get with the program."

Cheryl shook her head. "I can't Mr. Sla—"

He slapped his hand down on his desk. "My name is Joe."

"Sorry, I can't Joe. Even if I wanted to, my husband is liable to drop in at any moment and I'd have to quit."

"Tell me, how much you make a night."

Cheryl lifted her chin. "One hundred on a weeknight, two hundred on Friday and Saturday.

Joe picked up the handset of his phone and dialed a single digit. "Jack, it's Joe. Is Syn handy?"

"How about Mercedes?"

"Send her into my office, would you."

The door opened and Mercedes, a beautiful raven haired, Hispanic girl, stepped in. "Whoa, I see you got Princess prissy in here. Jack said you wanted to see me. What do you need?"

"Tell Cheryl what you made last Saturday."

"That depends."

"No whoring, Cheryl is a respectable married lady. Just drinks, tips and lap dances."

Mercedes scratched her head. "If I remember right it was between six and seven hundred, but Friday was better."

"How much better?"

"Two bills."

Joe's eyes widened. "You made between eight and nine hundred?"

She nodded.

"God, that's more than I make. Sometimes I wish I had tits and a pussy. Tell Cheryl what your best weekday was last week?"

"Three-fifty on Tuesday, but Syn claimed she made five hundred that night."

"Thanks Mercedes. You can leave now."

"Thanks," She turned to Cheryl. A little advice to you. I know you do your job, and I understand you are a newlywed, but if you're not going to take it off, at least get your nose out of the air."

Cheryl frowned. "What do you mean?"

"Stop acting like your shit doesn't smell. You know, if I had your face and body, I'd make six grand a week."

Mercedes opened the door and walked out.

Cheryl flared her nostrils. "Are we done?"

"Not quite. I have to get something out of you. Do you think you could at least give lap dances?"

"I don't know? Maybe."

"Well, you either do lap dances or I'll have to let you go."

"No topless?"

"No topless for now."

The Televangelist I

"All right. I'll do them. Can I go now?"

"Sure, go ahead. But come in early tomorrow. Since you're such good friends with Mercedes, I'll have her show you the ropes on lap dances."

* * * *

"Jamie Lee."

Jamie Lee felt someone shaking him.

"Jamie Lee, wake up. I have to leave."

Jamie Lee sat up and rubbed his eyes. Missy stood there looking like a million bucks, with a large suitcase resting beside her. He glanced at the clock. "It's 6:30 in the morning. Where are you going?"

She sighed. "I told you days ago I would be attending The Evangelical Woman's Society conference in Chicago and needed to leave early today."

Jamie Lee searched his memory. "That's right. How long did you say you'd be gone?"

"'Til Friday night. You could pick me up at the airport at five p.m. if you'd like."

"I might do that. Have a nice trip."

"Thank you. I'll call you with details about when I'll be in. I wouldn't have woke you except Marie will be here at eight. Let her in and when she's done, write a check, would you?"

He squinted his eyes and stuck his arms out wide. "For you, I would do anything."

She smiled. "You're such a ham." Stepping up to him with puckered lips, she kissed him. "I hear the cab honking. I gotta run. You be a good boy while I'm gone now."

"Always."

The Televangelist I

Jamie Lee tried to go back to sleep, but his mind seemed to work in overdrive.

Jamie Lee's ego was stratospheric. With each SOL telecast, his popularity grew. He'd become a full-fledged celebrity in the South Central states and the rest of the nation started to take notice of the handsome, charismatic televangelist.

Though he received plenty exercise in elevators and between the sheets, he decided to start working out in Missy's world-class fitness room. Sliding out of bed, he threw on shorts and shoes and headed to the work-out room. Until then his only work outs in there had been fucking Missy. He started with the oar machine then moved to the treadmill. After an hour, he took a shower and started to get ready for work when the fancy door chimes rang. Maria! Standing there naked while brushing his teeth he rinsed his mouth and threw on a robe. Then he padded to the front door and let Maria in.

Oh yeah, he remembered Maria. Nice, very nice. "Hi Maria. Won't you come in?"

Maria stepped in and glanced around. "Where is Miss Riverton?"

"She caught a plane this morning for Chicago, where she will be until Friday."

The way Maria eyed him, there was an attraction between them and they both knew it. "Ah, so you are a, how you say, bachelor for three days?"

He smiled and plucked his forefinger on her pert nose. "Something like that."

Maria scanned his attire and seemed to hold back a laugh. "Too lazy to dress for the maid, huh, *Senor?*"

He returned the favor by looking her up and down. Long curly black hair, warm brown eyes and full kissable lips in a shapely, tight, five-four package, dressed in jeans and a tee shirt—no bra. "Not at all. I was brushing my teeth, standing there naked, when the doorbell rang, so I just threw on a robe to answer the door."

Maria looked amused as a solo eyebrow rose. "Ah, so you sleep *en el desnudo.*"

Jamie Lee grinned. "My grandmother is Mexican, so I know what that means."

She looked pleased. "Ah, so you are part Mexican. So, do you?"

Jamie Lee nodded. "What? Sleep naked. Yes, sometimes. I do lots of things naked, swim, bathe, shower."

"I'll bet." Her gaze lowered to his bare feet and back to his crotch, which had tented. Her intense gaze returned to his eyes. "What is the favorite thing, you like to do naked?"

"Honestly?"

She edged up to him so close his growing erection pushed into her midriff. In a sultry voice, she whispered in his ear. "Hon-est-ly."

"I like to make love to a beautiful woman."

"*Fantástico.* Are you a *grande romancero.*"

He laughed. "I like to think so."

"You like Maria?"

He looked her up and down. "Very much."

The Televangelist I

"I like you too. Very handsome." She grabbed his hand. "You take Maria in bedroom?"

Jamie Lee's libido along with his ego knew no bounds. His star was rising and there was no stopping him. The only problem he saw was his obsession for sex. And not just one girl. He had a wandering eye. He had to rein it in—if he could. "I would love to Maria—truly—but I mustn't. Missy and I are engaged to be married."

"But I thought—"

Her mouth remained open as he went on, "You go ahead and get started, I need to get ready for work. Let me know when you're finished so I can pay you."

Jamie Lee left Maria and went back in the bedroom to get ready for work when his cell phone with the private number rang. *Who could that be?* "Hello?"

"Tahiti was nice, but I could have used some company."

"Dan-n-y...are you back?"

"Almost. The cruise ship just pulled into port in LA. After I catch my flight at eleven–thirty, allowing for the two hour difference in time, I should arrive at DFW Airport between four thirty and five."

"How was the cruise?"

"Oh, it was nice all right, but I have to tell you, I've thought about you the whole time I was gone. I can't wait to get you alone, so I can...interview you."

"Me too. I thought of you. Do you need a ride when you get in?"

"That would be great. Let me call you with the time, gate, and terminal."
"Great. I'll be waiting."
So much for reining it in.

The Televangelist I

Chapter Sixteen -

*I know me, and those close to me know me. But sadly,
the outside world thinks I'm some kind of a crook.*
Rev. Benny Hinn

Driving to the office in his hundred thousand
dollar Mercedes, Jamie Lee felt good. Everything was
going better than he could have wished for. He spent at
least ninety minutes a day devouring all news about
himself, Soldiers of the Lord, or television ministries in
general. As he pulled onto the freeway his ringing
handheld phone interrupted his thoughts. "Hello?"

"It's me baby. I just got off the plane at O'Hare
Airport."

"Oh, hi."

"Did you let Maria in?"

A slight pang of guilt passed through him for
wanting Maria. "Yes, she was cleaning when I headed
for the office."

"Good, she's a good girl."

"Seems like it. I wrote a check for her before I
left."

"Thank you. I'm sure going to miss you for the
next four days."

"Me too."

She laughed. "Just make sure you behave yourself while I'm gone."

Another pang of guilt. "What do you mean? I wouldn't do anything."

"Gee, I know you wouldn't. I'm just in a randy mood because of what I did on the plane."

"What was that?"

"Ahh, I hope you don't think poorly of me, but on the flight, I joined the mile high club."

Jamie Lee frowned. "You did? Who with?"

"You, or rather your image. I always wanted to and I was thinking of you so I thought what the heck."

He laughed, "Good for you. We'll have to do that for real in the church jet."

"Yes, if we don't do it sooner we could do it on our honeymoon, when they fly us to Paris."

"Perfect. I have to go now."

"All right I just wanted you to know I arrived. I love you."

"I love you too."

* * * *

Gwen looked up and smiled. "Hi."

She wore a low cut vermillion dress and had her hair partially up with ribbons and a hairpiece. Mmm, she looked good. "Hi, did the reverend get off?"

Gwen giggled. "Boy, if that isn't a leading question. I'm sure with your mother's help he gets off a lot."

Jamie Lee frowned. "That's not what I meant and you know it. How did you know about them?"

The Televangelist I

"Oh, starting about two or three weeks ago, she occasionally came in here. She tried to look in on you too, but you weren't in. Anyway, if I didn't suspect anything by that, the way your mother comforted him and the way he glommed onto her at the funeral was a giveaway. She's very pretty, your mother, young too. Was she a teen mother?"

"Thank you. Yes, she was."

Anyway, if that wasn't enough to figure out there was something going on between them, the boss, told me he was taking her to Vegas."

Jamie Lee's brows elevated. "Did he now?"

"Uh-huh. He also left me some instructions to give to you?"

"Really. Where are they?"

"They're verbal. Sonny says while he's gone, you are supposed to give me three orgasms per day."

He laughed. "Is that why you're all fixed up today?"

"Yep. Except, I forgot one thing."

"What's that?"

"Before I tell you, let me tell you my fantasy.

"Every day I sit here and if I'm not answering the phone or typing, I stare straight at those elevator doors. Usually, the doors are closed, but sometimes they open and one or more persons step out. It never bothered me until you became one of those persons. Then every time they opened, no matter who emerges, I'd picture us together. I'm wearing this dress and your arms are wrapped around me. My back is bent backward, the front of my dress rests on my right leg, which wraps around you while your lips suck on my nipple and obviously your dick is buried in me."

Jamie Lee threw his head back and laughed. "And the thing you forgot..."

"Was my panties."

Jamie Lee walked around Gwen's desk. "I feel like dancing to elevator music. If we're lucky they may play a tango."

Twenty minutes later, they stepped off the elevator, arm in arm. Gwen blew air upward out of her beautiful lips, which rustled her red hair. "Phew! Did you like it?"

"I did. If I weren't such a visible person, it would have been exciting to ride the elevator down to the lobby and back. You know? The risk of discovery."

Gwen, apparently liking the idea arched her brows. "We could wear masks?"

"We could, couldn't we? I'll think about it. For now, let me go in my office and make a couple calls, before we work on orgasm number two. Bring me a cup of coffee when you get a chance."

Jamie Lee went around his large desk, picked up the handset, and dialed the number with his other hand.

"Hennings."

"Hi Mike. This is Jamie Lee Vincent. I got your number from Sonny."

"Of course, Jamie Lee. What can I do for you?"

"Don't suppose I could tell you in person."

The Televangelist I

"Of course, it's about time I meet you anyway. How's tomorrow at two sound?"

"See you then."

* * * *

It was eleven-thirty when Danielle called.

"Hello?"

"I'll be arriving at Gate A-26 at four-forty."

"What terminal?"

"Sorry, terminal A."

"I'll be there."

At three-fifteen Jamie Lee told Gwen he was leaving and headed out.

He arrived at terminal A at four twenty, parked in the short-term parking and sauntered into the terminal. Ten minutes later, he arrived at Gate A26 and watched as the Boeing 737 docked. He hoped he'd recognize her. He couldn't quite remember what she looked like, other than she was gorgeous. After all, he'd only seen her for about fifteen minutes total, over a month ago. The minute he saw her short, peach skirt swaying with the motion of her hips as she sashayed up the boarding bridge, his memory came flooding back. *She is absolutely stunning. I have to have this woman!*

A broad smile embellished her lovely face when she saw him. She shifted into a brisk almost shuffle-like walk and rushed up to him. When she stood in front of him, he grabbed her arms in a light embrace.

She kissed his cheek. "How have you been?"

"I've been fine. I forgot how absolutely stunning you were."

Beaming, she kissed him again. "You sir, are nothing but a charming flatterer, still I love it. Are you ready to go?"

"I am. Lead the way."

After they claimed her three large suitcases and make-up case, they engaged a porter, who loaded the luggage into Jamie Lee's car when he pulled into the loading zone. After helping Danielle into the passenger seat, Jamie Lee handed him a ten.

The porter said, "Thanks," Then studied him with narrowed eyes. "Hey, aren't you – "

"No, I just look like him."

Jamie hopped in the driver's seat, put the car in drive, and off they went. "Are you hungry?"

"Not yet. Maybe after you take me home."

"Is that where you're going to interview me?"

"I hadn't thought about it, but it works for me."

Danielle lived in a nice two-bedroom apartment in a large upscale Fort Worth apartment complex. After lugging the heavy suitcases up the stairs and into the second floor dwelling, Jamie Lee relaxed on the divan while she changed into something more comfortable.

Waltzing out in designer jeans, a sleeveless white blouse and wedge heeled sandals, with her hair in a pony tail, Danny looked like a teenager – albeit a hot teenager. He decided she still looked good enough to eat, but he barely recognized her.

Tucking one leg under the other, she sat in the loveseat across from him. She sighed. "That's much

The Televangelist I

better. You know I really loved my trip, but there really is no place like home.'"

"Are you hungry yet?"

She pursed her lips. "I am, but I don't feel like going out. I have a suggestion."

"Yes?"

Her pursed lips moved to the side. "How about if I order some Chinese take-out and while I get ready for the interview, you go get it?"

He raised his hands and shrugged. "Sounds good to me."

Twenty minutes later, admiring her shapely derriere, Jamie Lee followed Danny into the kitchen to prepare their plates and drinks.

Returning to the living room, they reclaimed their seats. Between bites, Danny placed a recording device on the cocktail table and explained, "Rather than take notes, where errors can occur, I'll record the interview. Do you mind?"

He raised his hand and flipped out his fingers in a disinterested manner, "That's fine."

"Good..." She swallowed. "Now, I'll sift through what you tell me and write my story from there, so if you tell me, accidently or on purpose, anything you wouldn't want revealed, tell me it's off the record. Okay?"

"Understood. I have something I'd like to tell you off the record."

One of her brows dipped while the other rose. "Really, what is that?"

The Televangelist I

Jamie Lee smirked, "That, I'd love…to eat your pussy…then fuck you."

Her mouth fell open and she fidgeted. Her eyes followed him as he moved over beside her, but she seemed speechless.

Sidling in beside her, he took a deep breath. "I love that perfume. What is it—lilacs?

In a soft sultry voice she responded, "Gardenias. Sweetheart, I'm super attracted to you, too, but you just got engaged."

Ignoring her comment his mouth nuzzled into the crook of her neck peppering it with moist kisses. "You're so hot; I'll bet your kisses taste like Tabasco flavored honey."

With closed eyes, she elevated her chin, exposing more of her neck for his attention. As his lips worked their way up toward her ear, she groaned.

Hard as a brick, Jamie Lee brought her hand to his hardness, then whispered in her ear, "Look what you do to me. I want you bad—more than I've wanted any woman."

Quavering, she pushed her left breast against his shoulder, as she wrapped her long fingers around his neck. In a shaky, breathy manner, she cooed, "Really? What would your fiancé think about that?"

She gasped as his left hand slipped over one thigh, his fingers dipping in between her legs. As he massaged where they joined, a long, low moan issued, from her throat.

"She's merely going to be my wife. I want you to be *my* mistress. I want to take you in that bedroom, spread your legs and devour you. When you scream for mercy, I will ravish you. I will make love to you like no one has or can!"

Danielle rose and looked down at Jamie Lee. His hand, which had been between her legs, wrapped around her as she stood and rested on her round firm ass. She reached behind her, grasped it, and tugged it upward. "I think we should take a break from the interview."

He smiled and rose. Taking her in his arms, his lips covered hers in a passionate kiss as his left arm slid behind her legs, lifted her, and carried her into the bedroom.

* * * *

The next morning, Jamie felt like he was on top of the world. "Hi beautiful."'

A bright smile spread across Gwen's face. "Hello, Mr. Vincent." She raised a pair of Mardi Gras style masks. "Look what I brought."

Jamie Lee smiled and wagged a solitary finger. "You *are* a naughty girl."

Her smile closed to a tight-lipped grin. "I have a great instructor."

He laughed. "What are you going to do about your bright red hair? It's a dead giveaway."

Arching her eyebrows, she put down the masks and raised a blonde wig.

Jamie Lee smiled and asked, "Bring me coffee, will you?"

"Yes sir, but take your messages. There's a very interesting one. I put it on top."

Taking the slips of paper Gwen handed him, he strutted into his office and sat at his desk. The first message was indeed interesting.

From: Jay Cummings from the Arslen Hall Show.

Message: Please call, 1-800-555-6222.

Gwen brought his coffee. Raising her eyebrows she said, "Here's your coffee. Is there anything else you'd like?"

Knowing what she had in mind, he held back a chuckle. "Yes."

She stared at him expectantly.

He handed her the Arslen Hall slip. "Get Mr. Cummings on the line for me, will you."

A pout formed on her lips. She snatched the paper, spun around and sashayed out of his office.

A short time later, the intercom rang. "Yes Gwen."

"Mr. Cummings is on line one."

"Thank you." Jamie Lee punched line one. "Hello Jay. I had a message you called."

"That's right. I line up guests for the Arslen Hall show and Mr. Hall said he thought you and the future Mrs. Vincent might make fascinating guests. Do you have any interest in becoming a guest?"

"I might. Tell me more."

"Yes. We would pay for your fiancé and your airfare and put you up at the five-star Beverly Wilshire Hotel. You wouldn't be paid much, union scale, but the exposure would be great for your ministry."

"Does it matter when?"

The Televangelist I

"No, whenever it's convenient, but we need to know a few weeks in advance."

"I am interested, but I need to ask Missy. If she doesn't want to do it, are you interested in just me."

"Oh yes. Arslen is primarily interested in you. His father was a Baptist minister, you know."

"No, I didn't know. I'll tell you what. Let me check with Missy and I'll get back with you."

A minute later, Gwen walked in with a cup of coffee and the masks she had shown Jamie Lee earlier. "Here's a refill. How did the call go?"

He glanced up at her. She was a blonde. He chuckled. "Hey, you look good as a blonde. Is that a hint?"

"Let's say it's a reminder. The call, how did it go?"

"It went good. They want Missy and me to be guests."

"I wouldn't guest with Missy the first time. She's too distracting. I think you should go on alone, and then come back in March with Missy, right after the wedding. You could re-enact the wedding, now that would bring an audience—the dream couple. I'll bet I could even get you on the Johnny Carter Show."

Jamie Lee swallowed. "You?"

"Sure, why not?"

"I think you might have something there. Let's get the Hall show under our belt and then give it a shot."

Gwen cocked her head and lifted up the masks. "Speaking of shots. I could use a shot of elevator love."

The Televangelist I

"All right. Just that. You'll have to come over to Missy's house tonight for the follow-up."

"That's right she's at a convention until Friday." A coy naughty look formed on her beautiful face. "Won't that be a kick? Fucking you in her bed."

* * * *

At two on the dot, Jamie Lee received a call on the intercom from Gwen. "Hello."

Gwen was so curt and formal, Jamie Lee wondered what was wrong. "Mike Hennings is here to see you."

"Thank you. I've been expecting him. Send him in."

Almost instantly, the door opened revealing a tall, fairly fit, middle-aged man. He smiled and stepped in, then walked up to Jamie Lee holding his hand out. "Mike Hennings. I handle security for the ministry."

Jamie Lee rose from his seat and leaned over to shake his hand. "Jamie Lee, Nice to meet you Mike. Sounds like a big job."

Mike sat in the closest chair. "You have no idea. I have to take care of the church, the corporate campus, which, as you know includes the studio, satellite offices, the missions, the airplanes, boats and helicopters, even the executive homes. Now there's talk of a college. What can I do for you son?"

"I want you to find an old school chum and his wife for me."

"Go on."

"You want to write this down or something?"

Mike smiled and pulled a miniature recorder from his coat pocket. "This will get it, proceed."

"His name is Tommy Parkson and hers is Cheryl, formerly Alpern."

"Spell both names."

"Tom—"

Mike signaled for him to stop. "Sorry, I meant both of her names."

"Oh. C-H-E-R-Y-L A-L-P-E-R-N."

"Thank you. Go on."

"All right. I'm pretty sure they live in Dallas or at least the Dallas/Fort Worth area."

"That would be helpful if they did. What do they do and when was the last time you saw them?"

"I saw them both at Michael's funeral. He's a TV cameraman or at least involved in TV. I think she just goes to college."

"You wouldn't happen to have a phone number?"

Jamie Lee shook his head. "I did have a number, but it was stored in my phone, which I smashed against the wall when something upset me."

He chuckled. "Sounds like you have a temper— like me. Anyway, that's all right. I have plenty of information to work from. Don't hold me to this, but I should be able to tell you anything you want to know about them in two or three days."

"Great." Jamie Lee rose and offered his hand across the desk. "Mike it's been a pleasure. Looking forward to your report."

The Televangelist I

Mike also rose and shook Jamie Lee's hand. "Likewise, and congratulations on your engagement, she is an exceptional looking woman."

Shortly after Hennings left, Gwen came in. "What did he want?"

"You don't like him, I take it. No. He creeps me out. Ever since Sonny brought me up here, he's been asking me out."

Jamie Lee pursed his lips. "What is your status with Sonny lately?"

"He's been leaving me alone lately. Your mother seems to have him all wrapped up. Just like you have Missy and me all wrapped up. There must be something in your family genes."

Jamie Lee laughed. "Let me ask you. What would you do if Sonny wanted to take you in his sleeping room again?

"I've actually worried about that. Even though he's more than double my age, he wasn't a bad lover, but now that I've sampled you, I'm not interested."

"That didn't answer my question."

"What would you think? Would it bother you?"

"Not at all. I don't love you."

The way her mouth parted and the sparkle left her eyes, it was obvious that wasn't the answer she wanted.

"Do you feel anything for me?"

He smiled. "I don't know if this will assuage your hurt feelings. But I like you a lot and I have an overpowering attraction to you."

"That helps. At least I don't feel used."

The Televangelist I

"No, don't ever feel used. You make me very happy."

Surprising him and probably herself, she kissed him. "Thanks for being honest with me. I had no illusions about us when we started, but the more we were together the more I thought it might work into something."

The Televangelist I

Chapter Seventeen – Babes Galore
If I do not return to the pulpit this weekend, millions of people will go to hell. Jimmy Swaggart

It'd only been two weeks since Cheryl had her talk with Mr. Slabova, when her new friend Mercedes came up her and told her the boss wanted to see her.

Cheryl slalomed around the tables, nervous as a virgin at Beltane, to Joe's office. Standing at the door, she took a deep breath and knocked.

"Come in."

She opened the door enough to stick her head in. "Mercedes said you wanted to see me."

"Yes, Cheryl thanks, have a seat. Please."

Cheryl took a seat in the only chair in the tiny office. The same beat up old chair she'd sat in two weeks previous. After crossing one leg over the other, she asked, "What do you want? I've been giving lap dances. I've given one already tonight."

He waved a hand. "Calm down. I know, I've been talking to the girls and they said you've been giving lap dances, but we still have the same problem."

Getting a bad feeling, Cheryl's nose scrunched.

Joe pushed his chair back as he stood. "Take your top off."

Cheryl's eyes rounded. "What!"

Joe frowned. "Take your top off. I want to see what the roosters are missing by you withholding the goodies."

Cheryl felt incredulous. "If I won't show the goodies for them, why should I show the goodies for you?"

"Because, I'm the boss and I say whether you stay or hit the road and right now you are at the door. Now, show me the fucking goodies."

She snarled. "I'm not going to fuck you."

Joe shrugged and lifted his hands up shoulder high. "Did I ask you to fuck me? Now take off your fucking top."

Cheryl reached behind and unclasped her top. Her hands came around to the front, and slowly she peeled the top down.

Joe gasped. "Oh my God. Those are magnificent. Sweetheart. How much are you making each night since you started giving lap dances?"

"About fifty more on week days, a hundred on weekends. Can I put my top back on now?"

"In a minute. I gotta tell you, with the rack you have, you could be making Three to four times that much, if you just weren't so shy."

Joe came around his desk and she gulped as he edged up behind her. Two rough hands slipped over her shoulders past her chest and kneaded her breasts.

She gritted her teeth and closed her eyes.

A whiff of musky cologne accompanied movement and then she felt moist lips sucking on one of her nipples.

She squirmed, but not because it felt awful. Soon his fingers began to diddle her other nipple and she grew warm—very warm. To her shame, she started to get turned on. Then to her relief, and maybe even her salvation, Joe pulled away.

"Your husband is a lucky man."

"Thank you."

Cheryl started to put her top on and Joe grabbed it. "What the fuck are you doin'?"

"I showed you my breasts, I even let you feel and suck them. I'm putting my top back on."

"Who made you boss? I'm trying to work with you. Believe me, I would dearly love to fuck you, or at least stick my dick down your throat. I've been a gentleman, because I can tell you are a nice lady. But I have a business to r—"

There was a short knock on the door. Then it opened and Bambi stepped in. "Oh, I'm sorry, I didn't..." She glanced at Cheryl. "I see you got Miss Prude to show her stuff. Ooh, nice hooters, I have to admit." She turned to Joe. "I'll come back later." Then she turned and left.

"Can I go now?"

"Are you gonna show your knockers?"

"Joe, I can't. What if Tommy comes in?"

"I'll tell you what? You give me a snapshot of your hubby, start taking your turn on stage and I'll take care of the rest."

"You want me to take my top off?"

"Two minutes. Just flash them beautiful boobs for two stinking minutes at the end of the third song.

The Televangelist I

That's all I ask and you'll triple what you're making. Is that so bad?"

"What about lap dances?"

"Yes they have to be topless, but, you can give them in the VIP room so your husband don't see you. Do this and I'll never bother you again."

"How about if I let you know tomorrow?"

He bowed his head and shook it. "Sure."

"Can I go now?"

"Why not."

She stood legs parted, arms akimbo and head cocked. "My top?"

A mischievous looking smile formed on his lips. "I'll tell you what. Step out of my office about ten feet and I'll throw the top to you."

"Promise."

"I promise."

"Okay." Cheryl stepped just outside the office and held her hands up in a catching position."

Standing in the doorway, Joe faked an underhand throw, then threw the balled up top overhand as far as he could. "Oops, sorry. I threw it too hard." He laughed as she ran after it."

Cheryl never got her top back. One guy picked it up and when Cheryl asked for it politely, he took one look at her breasts and threw it to someone else. This went on for ten minutes while she and her boobs bounced from one laughing creep to another. By the time she realized what was happening, some fifty guys had gathered around and were ogling her. She yelled,

"Fuck you," and walked away seething. But, seething wasn't the only emotion she felt. The admiration of so many men had gotten her worked up. Her bikini bottom was wet and a trickle of cream meandered down one thigh.

Mercedes saw what happened, and intercepted her on the way to the dressing room. "That was a shitty thing, they did."

"It was a shitty thing, Joe did?"

"That too. I have a spare suit I can loan you. Come with me."

Soon Cheryl emerged in a silver bikini.

Finally realizing the game was over, the man who'd ended up with her top handed it back to her. "I gotta tell you miss, you made my night. I love your face and body."

"Thank you." Since almost everyone had already seen her breasts she decided to take her turn on the stage and see how it went. When she had to do lap dances, she pretended she ground herself on Tommy's lap. She made five hundred that night—a Tuesday night.

How much I could make on Friday and Saturday. She couldn't wait to find out.

* * * *

That night in Missy's bedroom, Gwen stretched her arms and cast a smile of pure satisfaction. "Umm, that was wonderful. You are spoiling me for all other men. How come when we're in a bed, you start by going down on me?"

The Televangelist I

"Because when I see that patch of bright red hair down below, I want to devour you. What would you like to do now?"

"Well this is off topic, but you never answered my original question at the office."

Jamie Lee raised his brow. "Which was?"

"What did Mike Hennings want?"

"Your question should be, what did I want from him?"

She pursed her lips. "All right, what did you want from him?"

"I want him to find an old school chum of mine."

"Why?"

He frowned again "You sure are inquisitive tonight. Don't you want to make me feel good?"

"Of course I do. Just humor me."

"I'm going to ask him to be my best man."

"Oh." Gwen wrapped her fingers around him and began to stroke. "One more question and then I'm going to put your giant wiener in my mouth."

"Yeah?"

"Do you love Missy?"

He shook his head. "I try. Believe me I try. She's a wonderful girl who deserves to be loved, but I can't seem to get there."

"Then how do you feel about her?"

"The same as you. I like her a lot and she makes me feel real good."

"Okay, one more question and then I'll gobble your wiener. Do you love anyone?"

"My mother." *And Cheryl!*

* * * *

The door opened and a lean, tall, man, who appeared to be in his mid to late forties with a receding hairline, peeked out. "Who're you?"

"Mr. Miller, I'm Michael Hennings and I represent the Soldiers of the Lord ministries."

The man looked Michael over and then pulled the door open. "Come in."

Hennings stepped through the door and followed the man after he closed the door. The home a ranch style tract house was nothing special.

Miller pointed at a dilapidated couch and sat down in an equally run down chair. "Did you bring my money?"

Hennings sat down and smiled. "That's what I'm here to talk about."

"And?"

"SOL will not pay blackmail."

"I don't consider this blackmail. I can either straighten out the record or ignore it. My reputation has been denigrated and in order to ignore that I need incentive."

"Denigrated? That's a pretty big word for an appliance salesman and former hippie."

"I was a college professor at San Jose State University, before I formed my commune."

"And were you in the habit of raping sixteen year olds at your commune?"

Miller shifted in his seat. "I didn't rape her. She wanted it."

"Hmm." Hennings rubbed his chin. "Is that right? Then I guess these three commune members who signed affidavits stating you raped Consuela Vincent lied."

"I guess so."

"Well, at least one thing is indisputable. Consuela was sixteen and in California anyone having sex with a minor is committing statutory rape."

"What's your point?"

"My point is you mess with us, you end up one of two ways — in prison or the ground."

"What do you want?"

"We need to come to an agreement, 'cause, believe me, you don't want to see who comes after me.

"Hello."

"Charlie. It's Mike. I need you to tap some yokel in Racine, Wisconsin's home phone."

"Sure Bud. You want full time surveillance."

"No, for now tape it, voice activate, and check it daily."

"What are we looking for?"

"Contact with newspapers, media, publishers, lawyers, and while we're at it tap his phone at work too."

"You got it. Just give me the details."

* * * *

First thing Friday morning, Reverend Riverton walked in with a lilt in his step. "Good morning Gwen."

"Good morning sir. How was Vegas?"

The Televangelist I

"Glorious. Of course everything seems wonderful when you're in love."

"Aw, that's sweet." She raised an eyebrow. "Any plans?"

"Not anymore." Speaking *sotto voce* Sonny raised his hand to his mouth and said, "We got married."

"That's wonderful. Congratulations."

"Thank you. You need to find a nice man and fall in love yourself."

"I'd like that sir."

Just then, Mike Hennings walked in.

"Hi Mike are you here to see me?"

He nodded. "I'm afraid so."

Sonny raised his brow. "Bad news?"

Mikes lips tightened. "It ain't good."

Sonny waved for him to follow him into his office. "Come on in."

Following Sonny, Mike called Gwen's name just before going in.

He winked when she looked up. "Coffee, black."

Sonny leaned back in his chair and watched his security chief come in. "Have a seat Mike."

Mike sat in his usual chair, propped his feet on Sonny's desk, and clasped his hands behind his neck.

When he didn't say anything, Sonny asked, "What can I do for you?"

Mike appeared to be ready to answer when Gwen waltzed in with his coffee. Mike dropped his feet from the desk, sat up and took the cup. "Thanks Doll."

"You're welcome." Gwen scrunched her nose and left.

The Televangelist I

Mike stuck out his hand. "I overheard about your wedding, congrats. Your future son-in-law's mother, right?"

Sonny leaned over his desk and shook it. "Thanks. She's a wonderful woman."

"What about the redhead, are you gonna keep tapping that."

Sonny cathedraled his fingers. "If you got married, would you give Gwen up?"

"I guess not."

"That's enough small talk. What's this thing you came to see me about?

Hennings shifted in his seat and took a deep breath. "Your Racine problem has disappeared...literally."

Sonny leaned forward. "Can you find him?"

"Oh, we're working on it."

"And?"

Hennings shook his head. "Nothing yet."

"Well, find him and *eliminate* the problem."

"I know. We shoulda capped him to start with." He gritted his teeth. "This pisses me off. Give the guy a break and he skips out on us." Mike rose and grabbed his coffee cup. "Excuse me, I have to visit your son-in-law. Don't worry, I'll keep you informed."

* * * *

Jamie Lee heard a knock on his door. When he looked up, Mike Hennings stepped in, holding a cup. "You have time to see me?"

He waved Mike in. "Sure, have a seat. I'm glad you're here. I wanted to ask you a question."

The Televangelist I

Hennings took a seat. "Wha'cha need?"

"I'm starting to draw a lot of attention when I go out in public and not all of it is positive."

He nodded. "You need a bodyguard."

Jamie Lee leaned back in his chair. "That's what I was thinking, but not full time."

"Tell you what. I'll assign a guy to you and whenever you're going to go out in public, give him a call."

"That'll work. Thanks. Now, what did you want?"

A grin formed on Mike's face. "I found your couple, Tommy and Cheryl Parkson."

Jamie Lee leaned forward and crossed his arms on his desk. "You did?"

"Yeah, and, they're hard up."

Good. "That's too bad."

"Yeah, they live in a tiny apartment in Richardson. He had a job until three months ago, but was laid off and has been unemployed for three months."

"What about her?"

"Cheryl? She takes a few courses at a community college. Then last month she went to work at Babes Galore. I went and checked her out."

Jamie Lee tensed and a flash of anger shot through him.

"She's hot stuff. She has one of the best racks I've ever seen."

Fuming, Jamie Lee had an urge to take the handset of his phone and smash Mike's teeth out. He

The Televangelist I

knew his anger was unwarranted, but he couldn't help it. Mike'd seen Cheryl's breasts and he hadn't.

"Yeah, she's too classy for that joint."

"Anything else?"

"I think she's making pretty good money, but they're still way behind on their bills. Her car, the rent, utilities. You name it, they're behind."

"You wouldn't know who owns the place, would you?"

"Not for sure, but I got the impression, the manager, some Balkan dude named Joe Slabova also owns the place."

"Buy it!"

"What?"

"Buy the place. Let him manage it, but I want to own it."

"What if he wants an arm and a leg?"

"Make the best deal you can and buy the fucking place!"

* * * *

About ten minutes after Hennings went in Jamie Lee's office, Sonny felt strange. He became short of breath, dizzy and his extremities tingled. It scared the hell out of him, so he decided to go home. He slipped on his sport coat and went to tell Gwen he was leaving. "Gwen, I'm not feeling well, so I'm going home."

Looking away from him as she typed, she joked, "Yeah, I know how it is with newlyweds." Turning and looking at him, she realized her mistake. His skin blanched and his eyes glazed. "I'm sorry Sonny. Stupid joke. I can see you don't feel well."

"I understand. If I feel better by Monday, I'll be in. Otherwise don't look for me."

* * * *

As Sonny got on the elevator, Jamie Lee came out of the office. "What was that about newlyweds?"

Gwen smiled. "Sonny and your mother. Hadn't you heard? Looks like Cupid hit a bullseye. Isn't love wonderful?"

It was obvious, the way Jamie Lee's chin dropped, he hadn't known.

He sensed his jaw muscles tighten and his eyes narrow. "They got married?"

"I'm sorry, I assumed you knew. They got married and honeymooned in Vegas."

Jamie Lee walked back into his office and slammed the door so hard the wall cracked from the doorjamb to the ceiling. Jamie Lee was incensed. He wanted to confront them and ask why they had to sneak behind his back. Why they couldn't let him in on their plans.

* * * *

Connie was surprised to see Sonny walking through the front door. "Hello sweetheart, what are you doing home so early?" She joked. "Looking for a little afternoon delight?"

As he drew closer, she noticed he looked funny. He was pale and perspiration covered his brow. "Are you all right baby?"

"No, and sex is the last thing on my mind right now. I left the office because I feel terrible."

"What's wrong?"

The Televangelist I

He rubbed his chest. "I feel tight in here and I can't catch my breath." He looked frightened. Staring at Connie, he asked, "Baby, do you think I could be having a heart attack?"

He started to wobble so she ran up to him and wrapped an arm around him. "Sit down on the couch while I call your doctor and ask him."

"I think I'd rather get in bed. Could you help me into the bedroom?"

She nodded and started for the bedroom, but Sonny's eyes rolled back in his head and his legs gave out. With Connie's help, he collapsed slowly on the floor, where he seemed barely conscious. She ran to the phone and punched in 911, and then Connie watched helplessly as Sonny started convulsing and spitting up.

* * * *

"Yes, Gwen."

"Your mother is on line one and she sounds half hysterical."

"Thank you." He pushed line one. "Yes, Mom."

"I'm at Baylor University Medical Center. I need you here as quick as possible."

"I'm on my way. Are you all right?"

"I'm fine. It's Sonny. I think he's had a heart attack!"

To be continued in Book II

Coming Soon

The Televangelist I

Book II Of The Televangelis

This book is a work of fiction. Names, characters, places, and incidents either are products of the author's imagination or are used fictitiously. Any resemblance to actual events or locales or persons, living or dead, is entirely coincidental. All sexually active characters in this work are eighteen or older.

The Televangelist I

The Televangelist I